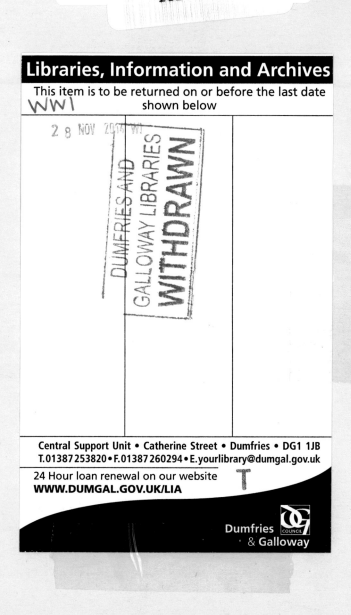

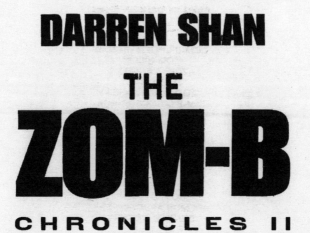

DARREN SHAN

THE ZOM-B

CHRONICLES II

SIMON AND SCHUSTER

First published in Great Britain in 2014
as an omnibus edition entitled ZOM-B CHRONICLES II
by Simon and Schuster UK Ltd
A CBS COMPANY

ZOM-B CITY first published in Great Britain in 2013
by Simon and Schuster UK Ltd
Text copyright © 2013 Darren Shan

ZOM-B ANGELS first published in Great Britain in 2013
by Simon and Schuster UK Ltd
Text copyright © 2013 Darren Shan

1 3 5 7 9 10 8 6 4 2

Simon & Schuster UK Ltd
1st Floor, 222 Gray's Inn Road
London WC1X 8HB

Simon & Schuster Australia, Sydney
Simon & Schuster India, New Delhi

A CIP catalogue record for this book
is available from the British Library.

Paperback ISBN: 978-1-47112-457-0
eBook ISBN: 978-1-47112-458-7

Printed and bound by CPI Group (UK) Ltd, Croydon, CR0 4YY

www.simonandschuster.co.uk
www.simonandschuster.com.au

THE

ZOM-B

CHRONICLES II

ZOM-B CITY

For:
Mrs Shan!!!

OBE (Order of the Bloody Entrails) to:
Elisa Offord – queen of the mutant babies

Edited in a swanky city apartment by:
Venetia Gosling
Kate Sullivan

Darren Shan is represented by
the urban ladies and gentlemen
of the Christopher Little Agency

THEN ...

A man with owl-like eyes visited Becky Smith one evening and told her there were dark times ahead. A few days later zombies attacked her school and one of them ripped B's heart from her chest. But because the zombies didn't eat her brain, she came back to life soon after her death, as a monster.

Most zombies were unthinking killing machines, but some regained their senses and became revitaliseds, undead creatures who could reason as they had before they died. But to stay that way, they needed to eat human brains. Otherwise they regressed and became savage reviveds again.

Months after her transformation, B recovered her mind. She was being held prisoner in an underground complex, guarded by a team of scientists and soldiers. She was part of a group of revitalised teenagers. They called themselves zom heads. When B refused to cooperate with her captors, all of the zom heads were denied brains as a punishment.

Shortly before the teenagers lost control of their senses, a nightmarish clown and a pack of mutants invaded the complex. The clown's name was Mr Dowling. B had never seen him before, but she had crossed paths with a few of the mutants.

Mr Dowling's followers uncaged the zombies and slaughtered any humans they could lay their hands on. The zom heads made a break for freedom. When one of them was found to be a living boy who had been disguised as a zombie, the others ripped his brain from its skull and tucked in. Only B resisted.

As B mourned the loss of her friend, a soldier called Josh Massoglia tracked down the zom heads and instructed his team to burn them to the bone. But for some reason he spared B and let her go. Weary and close to her conscious end, she staggered through a tunnel, out of the darkness of the underground complex, into daylight and a city of the living dead.

NOW . . .

ONE

The sunlight is blinding to my undead, sensitive eyes. I try to shut my eyelids, forgetting for a moment that they stopped working when I was killed. Grimacing, I turn my head aside and cover my eyes with an arm. I stumble away from the open door and the nightmare of the underground complex, no idea where I am or where I'm going, just wanting to escape from the madness, the killing and the flames.

After several steps, my knee strikes something hard and I fall over. Groaning, I push myself up and lower my arm slightly, forcing my eyes to focus. For a while the world is a ball of lightning-sharp whiteness. Then, as my pupils slowly adjust, objects materialise through the haze. I ignore the pain and turn slowly to assess my surroundings.

I'm in a scrapyard. Old cars are piled on top of one another, three high in some places. Ancient washing machines, fridges, TVs and microwave ovens are strewn around. Many of the appliances have been gutted for spare parts.

A few concrete buildings dot the landscape, each the size of a small shed. I came out through one of them. I guess that the others also house secret entrances to the underground complex.

I pick my way through the mess of the scrapyard, steering clear of the concrete sheds, ready to run if any soldiers appear. I still don't know why I was allowed to leave when the others were killed. Maybe Josh felt sorry for me. Or maybe this is part of a game and I'm going to be hauled back in just when I think that freedom is mine for the taking.

A stabbing pain lances my stomach. I wheeze and bend over, waiting for it to pass. The ground swims in front of my eyes. I think that I'm about to lose consciousness and become a full-on zombie, a brain-dead revived. Then my vision clears and the pain passes. But I know it's only a short respite. If I don't eat some brains soon, I'm finished.

I search for an exit but this place is a maze. I can't walk in a straight line because it's full of twisting alleys and dead ends. It feels like I'm circling aimlessly, trapped in a web of broken-down appliances.

I lose patience and climb a tower of cars. On the roof of the uppermost car I steady myself then take a look around, shielding my eyes with a hand. Exposed to the sunlight, my flesh starts itching wherever it isn't covered, my arms, my neck, my face, my scalp, my bare feet. I grit my teeth against the irritation and keep looking.

The scrapyard feels like a cemetery, as if no one has been through it in years. I came out of one of the secondary exits. The main entrance must be housed elsewhere, maybe in a completely different yard or building. I'm glad of that. I don't want to run into Mr Dowling or any of his mutants as they're trotting back to wherever it is they hailed from.

The yard is ringed by a tall wire fence. I spot a gate off to my left, not too far away, maybe fifteen metres as the crow flies. I start to climb down, to try and find a path, then pause. One of the concrete sheds is close by and there are a few piles of cars between that and the fence. If I leap across, I can get to the gate in less than a minute.

I gauge the distance to the shed. It's leapable, but only just. If I don't make it, the ground is littered with all sorts of sharp, jagged cast-offs which could cut me up nastily, even . . .

I grin weakly. I was going to say, *even kill me*. But I'm dead already. It's easy to forget when I'm walking around, thinking the way I always did. But I'm a corpse. No heart – that was ripped out of my chest – and no other properly functioning organs except for my brain, which for some reason keeps ticking over. If I misjudge my jump and a pole pierces my stomach and drives through my lungs, what of it?

11

I'll just prise myself free and carry on my merry way. It will hurt, sure, but it's nothing to be scared of.

I back up, spread my arms for balance, then race forward and jump. I expect to come up short, or to just make the edge of the roof. But to my shock I overshoot it by three or four metres and come crashing back to earth with a startled shriek. My fall is broken by a stack of dishwashers, which scatter and shatter beneath the weight of my body.

Cursing, I pick myself up and glare at the shed. I didn't do much leaping around when I was captive underground. It seems the muscles in my legs are stronger than they were in life. I think I might have just broken the women's long-jump record. B Smith — Olympic athlete!

I climb on to the roof of the shed and jump to the next set of cars, putting less effort into the leap this time. I still sail over my target, but only by a metre. Next time I judge it right and land on top of an old Datsun, a short hop away from the gate.

I stare around uneasily before getting down. I'm expecting soldiers to spill out of the sheds, guns blazing. But I appear to be all alone in the yard.

At the gate I pause again. It's a simple wire gate and it isn't locked. But maybe it's electrified. I stick out a wary hand and nudge the wire with one of the bones jutting out of my fingertips. The gate swings open a crack. Nothing else happens.

One last glance over my shoulder. Then I shrug.

'Sod it,' I mutter and let myself out, slipping from the scrapyard into the silent, solemn city beyond.

TWO

The area outside the scrapyard is deserted. Old boarded-up houses, derelict for years. Faded signs over stores or factories which closed for business long before I was born. The only thing that looks halfway recent is the graffiti, but there's not even much of that, despite the fact that this place boasts all the blank walls a graffiti artist could dream of. It feels like a dead zone, an area which nobody lived in or visited any time in living memory.

I stagger along a narrow, gloomy street, seeking the shade at the side. The worst of the itching dies away once I get out of the sunlight. My eyes stop stinging too. The irritation's still there but it's bearable now.

Halfway up the street, the stabbing pain in my stomach comes again and I fall to my knees, dry-heaving, whining like a dying dog. I bare my unnaturally long, sharp teeth and thump the side of my head with my hand, trying to knock my senses back into place.

The pain increases and I roll over. I bang into a wall and punch it hard, tearing the skin on my knuckles. That would have brought tears to my eyes if all my tear ducts hadn't dried up when I died.

My back arches and my mouth widens. I stare at the sky with horror, thinking I'll never look at it again this way, as a person capable of thought. In another few seconds I'll be a brainless zombie, a shadow of a girl, lost to the world forever.

But to my relief the pain passes and again I'm able to force myself to my feet, mind intact. I chuckle weakly at my lucky escape. But even as I'm chuckling, I know I must have used up all nine of my lives by this stage. I can't survive another dizzying attack like that. I'm nearing the end. Even the dead have their limits.

I stumble forward, reeling like a drunk. My legs don't want to support me and I almost go down, but I manage to keep my balance. Coming to the end of the street, I grab a lamp post and swing out into a road.

Several cars are parked along the pavement and a few have been stranded in the middle of the road. One has over-turned. The windows are all smashed in and bones line the asphalt around it.

The sun is blinding again now that I've left the gloom. I hurry to the nearest car in search of shelter. When I get there, I find two people lying on the back seat. Both boast a series of bite marks and scratches, each one of which is lined with a light green moss.

The zombies raise their heads and growl warningly. This is their turf and they don't want to share it with me. Fair enough. I don't really want to bed down with them either.

I lurch to the next car but that's occupied too, this time by a fat zombie who is missing his jaw — it was either ripped off when he was killed, or torn from him later. He looks comical and creepy at the same time.

The third car is empty and I start to crawl in out of the light, to rest in the shade and wait for my senses to crumble. To all intents and purposes, this car will serve as my tomb, the place where B Smith gave up the ghost and became a true member of the walking dead.

But just as I'm bidding farewell to the world of the conscious, my nostrils twitch. Pausing, I pull back and sniff the air. My taste buds haven't been worth a damn since I returned to life, but my sense of smell is stronger than ever. I've caught a whiff of something familiar, something which I was eating for a long time underground without knowing what it was.

Three cars further down the road is a Skoda, the source of the tantalising scent. As weary as I am and as agonising as it is, I force myself on, focusing on the Skoda and the sweet, sweet smell.

My legs give out before I get to the car, but I don't let that stop me. Digging my finger bones into the asphalt, I drag myself along, crawling on my belly like a worm, baking in the sun, half-blind, itching like mad, brain shutting down. Every part of me wants to give up and die, but the scent lures me on, and soon I'm hauling myself into the Skoda through the front passenger door.

The driver is still held in place by her seat belt, but is lying slumped sideways. Most of her flesh has been torn from her bones, and her head has been split open, her brains scooped out and gobbled up by the zombies who caught her as she was trying to flee. She's not entirely fresh but she's not rotting either. She must have been killed quite recently.

I should feel sympathy for the woman and curiosity about how she survived this long and where she was headed when she was attacked. But right now all I'm concerned about is that those who fed on her didn't scrape her dry. Bits of brain have been left behind. Slivers are stuck to her scalp and meatier chunks rest inside the hollow of her skull.

Like a monstrous baby taking to the teat, I latch on to the shattered bones and suck tendrils of brain from them. I run my tongue the whole way round the rim, not caring about the fact that it's disgusting, that I'm behaving like an animal. In fact I'm ecstatic, getting an unbelievable buzz from the grey scraps, feeling myself strengthen as I suck, knowing I can keep the senseless beast inside me at bay for a while longer.

When I've sucked the bones dry, I pull back a touch, wipe my lips, then steel myself for what I have to do next. 'For what I am about to receive...' I mutter, trying to make a sick joke out of the even sicker deed.

Then I stick my fingers into the dead woman's head, scoop out every bit of brain that I can find, and stuff myself like a cannibal at Christmas.

THREE

Once I'm done dining, I lean out of the car and force myself to vomit. If I keep food inside my system, it will rot and attract insects. I've no wish to become a sanctuary for London's creepy-crawlies.

I pull back inside and shelter from the sunlight as best I can, staring glumly at the ceiling of the car, thinking about the underground complex, Rage killing Dr Cerveris and leaving us to our own devices, poor Mark being eaten, the zom heads being burnt alive. What a horrible, pointless mess, the whole bloody lot of it.

The road outside is deserted. Nobody moves. The zombies are lying low, hiding from the sun like me.

I'm itching all over. I scratch gently, careful not to slice through my skin with the bones sticking out of my fingers. I catch sight of my injured knuckles and peel some of the ruined flesh away from them. The damage isn't bad but I'm probably stuck with the wound for life. (Or whatever passes for life these days.) The hole in my chest where my heart was ripped out hasn't healed fully, so I don't think this will either. I'm dead. Your body doesn't regenerate when you're a zombie.

Still, I won't have to bear the open scars too much longer. Normal zombies can last as long as an ordinary person. Those of us who recover our senses aren't so lucky. Dr Cerveris told me that the brains of revitaliseds start to decompose once they fire up again. I've got a year, maybe eighteen months, then I'm toast.

The day passes slowly. I think about the past, where Mum and Dad might be now, if they're alive, dead or wandering the streets of London as zombies. I recall the attack on my school. I wonder about the freaky clown and his mutants, why they tore through the compound, slaughtering all in sight, but freeing the zombies.

I wish I could sleep and kill some time that way, but the dead can't snooze. We're denied almost all of the pleasures of the flesh. The only thing we can still enjoy is food — as long as it's brains.

'You had it easy,' I tell the corpse on the front seat, moving into the back as the sun swings round. 'A couple of minutes of terror and pain, then it was all over. You probably didn't think you were one of the lucky ones as your skull was being clawed open, but trust me, you were.'

The woman doesn't respond, but I go on speaking to her anyway, telling her my story, my thoughts, my regrets, my fears. It's the first time I've talked about my feelings since I recovered consciousness. There was nobody in the compound I could confide in. Mark was the closest I had to a friend, but I couldn't trust him completely. For all I knew he was working for the doctors, a plant. And in fact he was, only he didn't know about it until it was too late.

The dead are the best listeners in the world. The corpse takes it all in, never interrupts, doesn't criticise me, lets me waffle on for as long as I like.

Finally the sun dips and night falls on London. I feel nervous as I slide out of the car. I've no idea what to expect. The soldiers and scientists told me nothing about the outside world. I don't know how much damage the zombies caused when they went wild, or if the living managed to suppress them. By what I've seen on this road – the lack of activity, the silence, the zombies sheltering in deserted cars – I assume the worst. But I won't know for sure until I explore some more.

The other zombies come out as I do, free to move around without irritation now that the sun has set. They don't shuffle like movie zombies – they walk almost as freely as when they were alive – but you couldn't mistake them for the living. Their eyes are glassed over, bones stick out of their fingers and toes, their teeth are too big for their mouths, they sniff the air like dogs.

The fat guy I saw earlier gets a whiff of me and moves in closer, head twitching as he sniffs and listens. I let him come as close as he likes, curious to see what he'll do, if he can tell that I'm different to him.

Something must register inside his chaotic mess of a brain, telling him I'm not entirely the same, because he circles me warily, studying me with his cold, dead eyes.

'Take it easy, boss,' I grunt, pulling up my T-shirt to reveal the hole in my chest. 'I'm one of you, honest I am.'

The zombie growls when he hears me talking, then frowns when he spots the hole where my heart once rested. He peers into it for ages, as if he thinks it might be a trick. Then he turns away and goes looking for dinner elsewhere.

'We accept you, gooble-gobble ...' I murmur, remembering something Tiberius used to say. Then I press on, leaving my temporary shelter behind, to find out if London truly has become a city of the dead.

FOUR

The streets are mostly deserted and the only people I glimpse are zombies. They seem to be drifting aimlessly, sniffing the air, looking for living humans to feed on. Many groan or whine, scratching at their stomachs or heads, suffering hunger pangs. Some have accidentally clawed through to their guts or poked an eye out. They're pitiful beasts in this sorry state. They'd be better off properly dead, no doubt about it.

Lots of zombies stop me as I draw close. They can tell I'm not exactly the same as them, maybe by my scent or the way I move. In almost every case, their face lights up with excitement, then creases with doubt, then returns to blankness once they realise I'm dead like they are.

The reviveds become a nuisance after a while. If I try to push on without stopping to be examined, they get angry and snap at me. I'm pretty sure I could take any one of them in a fight – it shouldn't be too difficult to outwit a brain-dead zombie – but I don't want to spend the whole night scrapping. It's easier to stand still, let them give me the once-over, then move on when they lose interest.

To clarify my situation, I rip a hole in my T-shirt to expose the left half of my chest. That speeds things up a bit, but some still stop me to make absolutely sure I'm not one of the living. With all the interruptions, I make little headway. It's been about a couple of hours since I left the car, but I haven't gone far.

I spot a newsagent's and let myself in. It's dusty. Shelves have been knocked down, broken bottles litter the floor, the glass in a drinks cabinet has been shattered. There are a few newspapers on the counter, all dated the day of the zombie attacks, the world's last normal day. The cash register is open, notes lying undisturbed inside it. I guess money doesn't matter much any more.

The electricity is off but I can see fairly clearly. My eyes work well in the dark, better than they do in strong light.

I find a large *A to Z* and take it outside. I look for a street sign, then do a quick check in the book. I'm in the East End. I don't know this area well, but I'm not far from more familiar territory. It's probably pointless, but with nowhere else to head for, I figure I might as well go home. I doubt I'll find anyone there, but at least I'll be in more comforting surroundings.

I replace the *A to Z* with a smaller version and stick it in the back of my jeans. Then I set off in a north-west direction, picking my way through the streets, stopping whenever I'm challenged by one of the roaming dead.

I endure the stop-start process for another hour before I get sick of it. It'll take forever if I keep going like this. There has to be a better way and I think I know what it is. I could try a motorbike or car, of course, but I never learnt to drive, and anyway, the roads are cluttered with crashed vehicles.

I find a street packed with shops and go on a scouting mission. First I slip into a chemist's and hunt for eye drops. My eyes don't produce tears now, so I need to keep moistening them or they'll dry out and my vision will worsen. Once I've doused them, I load a bag with several bottles and look around, wondering if I need anything else. I think about bandaging over the hole in my chest, but it's not a medical necessity – apart from the green moss, I haven't seen any signs of infection – and besides, the open hole makes it easier for the walking dead to identify me as one of their own.

I move on and spot a hardware store. I spend a bit longer in this shop, testing a variety of tools, looking for weapons in case I have to fight at any point. The zombies haven't bothered me so far, but I can't rely on them leaving me alone forever. I know from the tests underground that they'll attack revitaliseds if they feel threatened. I don't plan on antagonising anyone, but sometimes things can just kick off. Better to be safe than sorry.

I settle on a hammer, a couple of screwdrivers and a chisel. Light, easy to carry and use, effective. I spend a long time among the drills, playing around with them, wincing at the shriek they make – my sense of hearing is much better than it was when I was alive – but loving their sheer ferocity. It would be cool to become a drill-packing zombie, but the bulky machines aren't practical, so in the end, reluctantly, I leave them behind.

A file, on the other hand, is vital, and I spend even longer testing out the goods in that section. My teeth are constantly growing and need to be filed back every day or two. Otherwise they'll fill my mouth and I won't be able to speak. When I find a file that does the job, I give all of my teeth a thorough going-over, then stick it in my bag, along with replacements, and mosey on.

Next up, a large department store. Zombies are patrolling the aisles, checking behind clothes racks, looking for any juicy humans they might have missed. They keep mistaking mannequins for living people. They jump on them, growling and howling, then realise their mistake and trudge away sullenly. I get a good laugh out of that, but lose interest after the seventh or eighth time and crack on.

I browse the racks, looking for clean jeans, a new T-shirt and a long-sleeved, heavy jumper. I tear a hole through the jumper and T-shirt to show the cavity in my chest, then pick up gloves and a nice leather jacket, one of the most expensive in the store. I dress in the middle of the shop, not bothering with the changing rooms. The zombies don't take any notice of me as I strip off. They're not interested in nudity, only brains.

I try on shoes once I'm comfortable in the clothes, but can't easily slip them on because of the bones poking out of my toes. Finally I grab a few pairs of socks and jam them over my feet, letting the bones stick out through the ends.

A good hat is the next item on my shopping list. I don't find anything that I like in the women's section, so I head to the men's department and spot an Australian cork hat. Once I've pulled off the corks and string, it's perfect — with its wide brim, it will shade my face and neck.

'G'day, mate,' I drawl in a terrible Australian accent, studying myself in a mirror. 'Looking good, sport.' I try to wink at my reflection, forgetting again that my eyelids don't work. I scowl, then laugh at my foolishness. 'No worries!'

I make my final stop by one of the sales desks, where sunglasses lie scattered across the floor. I root through and find a few which fit me and which I don't mind the look of. When I'm happy with my choices, I put three pairs in my bag and clip the other pair on to the neck of my jumper.

All sorted, I grab some magazines, return to the windows at the front of the store and lie down. I spend the rest of the night reading about showbiz stars who will never glitter again now that the world has gone to hell, glancing up every so often to watch the occasional zombie prowl past outside.

When dawn breaks and the streets clear, I get up, toss the magazines aside, slip on my glasses and hat, pull on my gloves and step out into the brightening day. My eyes tighten behind the shades but gradually adjust. They're not as sharp as they were in the darkness, but protected by the dark glasses, I can see OK.

I move into the middle of the road and stand bathed by the rays of the sun, to test whether or not they irritate me through the covering of my clothes. They do to an extent, and the itching starts again, but it's nowhere near as bad as it was. I can live with it, so to speak.

'Right,' I snap. 'The day is mine.'

And off I set through the empty streets, claiming them as my own. B Smith — queen of the city!

FIVE

In all honesty, it's not much of a city to be queen of. I used to think that London was one of the most exciting places in the world, always buzzing, always something going on. Now it's like walking through the world's biggest graveyard, and an ugly, messy one at that.

The battle between the living and the dead must have been apocalyptic. There are signs of chaos everywhere, broken windows, crashed cars, corpses left to rot outdoors. Many houses and shops are burnt out and fires still smoulder in some of them. In other places pipes have burst and streets are flooded.

There are bloodstains everywhere and lots of dried pools of vomit. The reviveds might not be as mentally clued-up as I am, but it looks like they figured out the vomiting part easily enough. I guess even the mostly senseless dead get a shiver at the notion of playing host to a brood of worms, maggots and the like.

The stench isn't as bad as I thought it would be, but it's fairly gross all the same, especially since my nose is more sensitive than it once was.

Birds, rats and insects are feasting on the vomit, blood and rotting flesh. They're enjoying the run of the city now that the zombies have withdrawn for the day. The more alert creatures scatter as soon as they spot me, the birds taking to the air, the rats vanishing down the nearest hole. Only the insects ignore me and go about their business uninterrupted.

The electricity supply varies from street to street. In some it's been cut off and every house is dead. In others it's as strong as ever, lights are on, static crackles from radios, TV sets flicker in shop windows. I consider checking the channels, to find out if anyone is alive and broadcasting, but I can do that later. I want to continue exploring on foot first, not waste the tranquillity of the daylight. I can channel-surf tonight when the zombies come out in force and I hole up.

I come to a butcher's shop, pause and stick my head inside. Slabs of dried-out meat lie rotting everywhere. A few scavenging flies crawl across the withered cuts, searching for bits that are still edible, but I think they'll struggle.

A pig's carcass hangs upside down from a hook. Its head has been clawed open. I stare at it thoughtfully. I'm guessing that a zombie ripped out the brain, which maybe means we can thrive on animal brains too. I thought only human brains would keep us going, but it's good news if we can absorb nutrients from animals as well — I'd much rather scoop clean the inside of a pig's head than a human's.

This might be why I haven't seen any larger creatures. With humanity out of the way, wild dogs and cats should have the run of the streets. But so far I've seen nothing but rats, birds and smaller specimens. Maybe the zombies killed and ate the brains of larger animals, and all of London's pets have either been butchered or scared off.

I'll have to swing by London Zoo at some point. It's probably been cleaned out already – or the animals will most likely have died of starvation – but maybe I'll be able to gain access to areas off-limits to normal zombies. The good thing about having a working brain is that you can read maps and search for keys to unlock doors, simple tasks which are beyond most of the undead.

As I turn away from the pig, I notice a small red z painted on the frame of the door, a tiny arrow just beneath it. I frown, trying to remember where I've seen something like that before. Then I recall Mr Dowling daubing my cheek with a mark just like this one.

I glance around nervously. Have the clown and his mutants been here? Might they be watching me now? Mr Dowling freaked me out big time, especially when he opened his lips and dropped a stream of living spiders over me. I don't want to hang around and risk another run-in with him.

Hurrying from the shop, I come to a set of traffic lights.

The electricity is working here and the lights are operating as normal. The red man is illuminated and I automatically stop, waiting for the light to change to green.

After a few seconds, I squint at the light, look left, then right. Nothing moves.

'Of course not,' I grimace. 'There's no traffic because everyone's dead. You're a bloody moron, B.'

I chuckle at my stupidity. Stopping for a traffic light in a city of the dead! I'm glad none of my friends lived to see that. Ignoring the red light, I step out into the road. I'm not far from my old neighbourhood. Another hour, maybe a bit more, and I'll be back on –

An engine roars into life. My head snaps round and I spot a car tearing towards me. It had been parked nearby. I'd seen people moving around inside, but figured they were zombies sheltering from the sun.

I figured wrong.

Before I can withdraw to the safety of the pavement, the driver turns on his headlights and I'm momentarily blinded, even wearing the sunglasses. Wincing, I turn my head away and shake it wildly, disoriented and in pain.

Then the car smashes into me and knocks me flying through the air, far down the middle of the road, which up until a few seconds ago seemed just as dead and unthreatening as any other in this ghost city of the damned.

SIX

I hit the ground hard and slide for a few metres before coming to a stunned stop. Shaking my head, I woozily get to my feet. No bones seem to be broken, but my elbows have been badly grazed and the back of my head is throbbing. I run a hand over my scalp. Lots of torn flesh but it doesn't feel too serious. The jacket and clothes I picked up earlier are ripped to shreds, but all things considered it could have been a lot worse.

Then the doors of the car open and as four men step out, I realise it's far too soon to be judging this a lucky escape.

The men are dressed in combats and black boots. Each totes a rifle and I spot smaller guns and hunting knives strapped to their legs and chests. They're smiling and laughing, not looking in the least afraid.

'She's up,' one of the men says. 'You must be losing your touch, Coley.'

'I'm not losing anything,' the man called Coley snaps. 'I was only doing about thirty when I hit her. Didn't want to finish her off too soon. Essex, you want first shot?'

'Don't mind if I do,' the man on my far left says and raises his rifle.

I dive for cover behind a nearby car as he fires. He curses and fires again, but only hits one of the wheels.

'You missed,' Coley hoots.

'No fair!' Essex shouts. 'They're not supposed to hide.'

'Not all of them stand still,' one of the other men says, and this guy speaks in a thick American accent. 'The survival instinct is still alive in some. Looks like we might have a real hunt on our hands, gentlemen.'

'You want to deal with her, Barnes?' Coley asks.

'No,' the American says. 'Let's give Tag a shot first. This is what we brought them along for.'

'What do I do?' the fourth man asks. He sounds nervous.

'Edge over to your right,' Barnes says, and I hear him creeping around to my left. 'I'll flush her out. As soon as she –'

I don't wait for him to give more orders. Keeping low, I race back towards the butcher's shop, catching the men by surprise. A couple yell with alarm and fire wildly. Bullets scream past but I keep going.

I'm close to the shop when one of the men hits the window with a bullet and it shatters. As glass sprays everywhere, I fling myself through the hole and roll across the counter before dropping to the floor and taking cover.

'Hellfire!' Essex shouts. 'Did you see that?'

'Careful, boys,' Barnes drawls. 'We've got a live one here. Relatively speaking.'

'How do you want to play this?' Coley asks. He sounds excited.

'That depends on these two,' the American says. 'Do you want to go in after her and risk the thrill of a close encounter, or would you rather we smoked her out?'

As they discuss tactics, I raise my head, get a fix on them, then scout around and pick up a hefty butcher's knife. This is why I came back here rather than flee down the road. I was a target out there, the tools I picked up earlier no use against a group of guys with guns. I hate being trapped like this, but at least I have a decent weapon now.

Shuffling backwards, I search for another way out. There's a door at the rear of the shop, but it's locked and I can't find the key. I hurl myself at the door, hoping to smash through, but it's made of metal and it holds. I only bounce off it, bruising my arm in the process.

'What's she doing?' I hear Tag cry.

'Maybe she's lost her head and is thrashing around,' Barnes says calmly. 'Or she might be trying to find another way out. Coley, swing round back and make sure she doesn't sneak away.'

'She wouldn't be smart enough to think of that,' Coley says.

'You'd be surprised,' Barnes grunts. 'Some are almost as cunning as they were in life.'

As Coley circles round, the American addresses the other pair. 'This is unusual but not unheard of. Some of these beasts are smarter than others. They recall routines and procedures in some dim corner of their foul, undead brain and act like they did when they were alive.'

'How dangerous are they?' Tag asks.

'All zombies are dangerous,' Barnes huffs.

'But if this one's more of a threat than most, shouldn't we back off and leave her be?'

'We're hunters,' Barnes says stiffly. 'We don't withdraw once we've engaged our prey. We have to see this through to the end. If you prefer, you can return to the car and wait for us there, but my advice is to stick together. Never forget that this is a city of the undead. There's safety in numbers. I can't protect you if you cut yourself off from the rest of us.'

'I didn't know it was going to be like this,' Tag grumbles.

'Quit whining,' Essex snarls. 'They told us it could turn nasty. We knew the risks coming in. This is all part of the fun, right, Barnes?'

'Sure,' Barnes says drily. '*Fun*. That's what we promised you guys and we won't let you down. Coley, you in place yet?'

'Got it covered,' Coley shouts.

'Then if you boys will give me a minute ...'

There's a long pause. I peer over the counter, trying to see what they're up to, but Tag and Essex start firing as soon as they spot my head. Ducking again, I curse and grab another knife, determined not to go down without a fight and maybe take one or two of these bastards with me.

'Come on,' I whisper, gripping the knife tightly. 'Meet me on my own turf. Let's see how useful your rifles are up close.'

But the American is obviously thinking the same way I am, because even as I'm willing them to advance, he yells a warning to the others, 'Clear!'

A couple of seconds later a bottle comes flying through the window. There's a burning rag sticking out of the top of it. I don't know much about weapons, but I know a Molotov cocktail when I see one.

The bottle smashes into the wall and flames billow from it, scorching the shop, roasting the flies, blackening the scraps of meat. I don't wait to be engulfed by the fire. I started moving the instant I caught sight of the bottle flying over my head. As the glass explodes and flames roar around me, I launch myself over the counter and shoot through the window like a human bullet propelled from the heated chamber of the store.

Crashing back to earth, pain flares in my feet and I see that my socks are on fire. Yelping, I toss the knife aside and slap out the flames, then tear off the smouldering socks. I'm so concerned about my feet that I blank out everything else. It's only when I hear a soft clicking noise that I pause, look up and realise that the barrels of three rifles are pointed directly at my head.

SEVEN

Nobody says anything and nobody opens fire. The American is slightly in front of the others, studying me coolly, the mouth of his rifle trained on the centre of my forehead. The other two look less sure of themselves. I think of diving for the knife, but I'm afraid that if I move, their trigger fingers will tighten instinctively and that will be the end of me.

'She's smart for a dead bird, isn't she?' Coley remarks, sauntering back into view, rifle slung across his shoulder, grinning viciously. His hair is cut short like a soldier's and he's wearing a pair of designer sunglasses. 'Seems almost a shame to kill her.'

'It's not really killing, is it?' Tag frowns. He's a thin man with a Scottish accent. Long hair tied back in a ponytail. 'I mean, they're dead already, so it's not like we're murdering anyone, right?'

'Don't worry,' Barnes murmurs, never taking his eyes off

me. 'This isn't a crime. Nobody will hold us accountable for what we do here. She looks like one of us but she isn't. She has less right to exist than an animal. It's elimination, not execution. Now, who wants to –'

'Screw you all!' I scream and every one of the men recoils with shock.

'Jesus!' Essex roars. 'She spoke! Did you hear that? She bloody *spoke*!'

'I heard,' Barnes growls. His dark brown eyes are hard. He's taller than the others, lean and muscular. He's the only one not wearing gloves. His black hair is shot through with streaks of grey and there's a bullet tucked behind his right ear.

'What the hell is she?' Coley asks. He doesn't look so relaxed now, and has trained his rifle on me too.

'I don't know,' Barnes says softly.

'Is she alive?' Tag asks.

'She can't be,' Essex snorts. 'Look at the hole in her chest.'

'But she spoke.'

'Maybe it was a reflex action,' Essex says.

'Reflex action my arse!' I shout and again they flinch. I push myself to my feet and glower at the astonished hunters. 'My name's Becky Smith. I'm a teenage girl. If you shoot me, you can bet a million pounds there are plenty of people out there who bloody *will* hold you accountable.'

Barnes blinks and lowers his rifle a fraction. 'Are you a zombie?'

'What does it look like?' I sniff, pointing a finger at the hole in my chest.

'Then how are you speaking?'

'Some of us can.'

'None that I've seen,' he counters.

I shrug. 'Maybe if you asked first and shot later ...'

'This is insane,' Coley mutters, circling me slowly, keeping well out of reach, nervously eyeing the bones sticking out of my fingers. 'Every zombie we've ever seen is a rabid, sense-less beast. There can't be an in-between state.'

'Well, there is. I'm proof of that.'

'There are others like you?' Barnes asks.

'Yeah.' Then I recall Mr Dowling, the mutants, the flame-throwers. 'At least, there *were* ...'

'Where are they?'

'I don't know. We were being kept underground. Most of the others were killed, maybe all of them. I got away but I think I'm the only one. The clown attacked and everything went crazy.'

I stop, aware that I'm making no sense.

'Who *kept* you?' Barnes asks.

'Soldiers. Scientists. They were studying us.'

'Soldiers?' Essex yelps. He looks around, edgy now. 'This sounds bad to me. If the military's involved ...'

'We're not doing anything they'd disapprove of,' Coley says quickly. 'We're zombie hunters, that's all, helping clean up the mess.'

'But we're not supposed to be here,' Tag mumbles.

'Only because it's dangerous,' Coley reassures him. 'They tell people to keep away because they want to stop fools being killed or turned into zombies. But nobody's going to give professionals like us any grief for coming in and shooting some of the buggers. We're saving them a job.'

'Still,' Essex says, pointing his gun away from me, 'I think we should split. I don't want to be caught here by the army. They might mistake us for zombies and open fire from afar. I want to leave now.'

'We came here to hunt,' Coley snarls. 'You both begged to join us. We didn't force you.'

'I know,' Essex says stiffly. 'But now I want to stop. Tag?'

'Hell, yes.' He lowers his rifle.

'Bloody amateurs.' Coley spits with disgust, then cocks an eyebrow at Barnes. The American hasn't budged. 'What do we do?'

'If there are soldiers in the area, Tag and Essex are right, we need to get out of here. We're breaking the law. They might let us go with a slap on the wrist. Or they might shoot us dead. We'd be fools to risk it.'

'Fair enough,' Coley sighs. Lowering his rifle, he pulls a handgun and aims it at my face.

'What the hell!' I roar, throwing myself to the ground.

'Coley!' Barnes yells.

'What?' he frowns. 'She's a zombie. It doesn't matter whether she can talk or not. She's one of them.'

'One of the undead, definitely,' Barnes agrees, 'but partially one of the living too. I don't know how she can respond, but she's more than a walking corpse.'

Coley laughs cynically. 'Not much more. I say we kill her. One less zombie is always a good thing.'

He takes aim again.

'This is murder!' I howl. 'I can talk! I can think! I used to go to school!'

I don't know why I shouted that last line. It just popped out.

'Hush now,' Coley purrs. 'One little bullet and all your worries will be behind you.'

'Hold,' Barnes barks. 'We're hunters, not killers. We mop up the dead, we don't execute the living.'

'She's a zombie,' Coley protests.

'But unlike any other we've encountered. She can reason. She can plead for her life. We don't have the right to kill someone who understands what we're doing.'

'Not a some*one*,' Coley sneers. 'A some*thing*. And you might be going soft in your old age, but I'm not about to lose focus. These bastards killed the people I loved. I won't stop as long as they're active and I don't give a damn if they can talk or not.'

Coley cocks his gun. Tag and Essex gawp like children. Barnes goes on staring at me.

'She said her name is Becky Smith,' Barnes says softly.

'I heard.' Coley shrugs. 'I don't care.'

'Have you ever killed something that could tell you its name?' Barnes presses.

'As it happens, yes,' Coley says. 'That didn't stop me then and it sure as hell won't stop me now. She's a bloody zombie! They're the bad guys, remember?'

'I don't know about good and I don't know about bad,' Barnes replies softly. 'Until a few minutes ago all that mattered to me was the living and the undead. I thought the world had been divided neatly along those lines and I operated accordingly. Now I see it's not so simple. I can't kill this girl. Even though she's missing a heart, she's too much like a real person.'

Coley stiffens. 'Are you saying you'll stop me if I try to shoot her?'

Barnes considers that. I start to smile. Then he says, 'No,' and my smile fades away to nothing.

Coley grins and takes final aim.

'I don't have the right to stop you shooting her,' Barnes adds. 'You're a free agent, I'm not your boss, you're not answerable to me. And maybe you're right — maybe she is a monster, and we have every right to cull her like a rabid hound. But if you kill her, I'll put a bullet through each of

44

your kneecaps and leave you here for the other zombies to pick apart come night.'

Coley does a double take. Barnes's expression doesn't change. If he's bluffing, he's got a first-rate poker face.

'You'd do that to me?' Coley asks softly. 'After all we've been through these last six months?'

'I'd have to,' Barnes says. 'In my view that would be the only appropriate response. If you feel you have to kill this girl, I won't stop you. But be aware of the consequences.'

'You'd choose a zombie over a friend?' Coley snarls.

'You're no friend of mine, any more than I'm a friend of yours.' Barnes smiles icily. 'We're just a couple of guys who hunt together.'

Coley weighs up his options. I can tell he'd love to put a bullet through Barnes's head almost as much as he wants to put one through mine. But the American has a lethal air about him. He's not someone you go up against lightly.

'Have it your way,' Coley finally snarls, holstering his gun. He heads for the car, not looking at any of the others.

'Head on back, boys,' Barnes says, nodding at Tag and Essex. In a daze they follow Coley to the vehicle and get in. Coley fires up the engine and revs it angrily. For a moment I think he plans to mow down the American. But Barnes never gives any indication that he's worried. And although the car rumbles forward a metre or so, Coley doesn't push things any further.

'You've had a lucky escape today,' Barnes says.

'Yes,' I gulp. 'Thank you.'

'In this city, you'd better hope you stay lucky,' he mutters, then backs up, keeping his rifle trained on me the whole way, until he gets into the car. As soon as the door slams shut, the car squeals past. The last thing I see of the hunters is an angry-looking Coley giving me the finger.

Then the car turns a corner and is gone, leaving me lying alone in the road, still trembling at my narrow escape.

EIGHT

I drag myself through the streets, limping, bruised, the flesh torn to shreds on my elbows and at the back of my head. I don't think any bones are broken, though I can't be certain. The pain isn't as bad as it would be if I was alive, but it's pretty damn excruciating.

I recall the look of hatred in Coley's eyes as I stumble along. Oddly enough, I don't blame him for wanting to kill me. I probably had that same look when I first saw a zombie. We're monsters, plain and simple. The dead can, by definition, have no automatic right to life.

I make slower progress than before, hampered by my injuries. It's dusk before I turn into the street where I used to live. Some of the keener or hungrier zombies have already come out of hiding and are on patrol. A few stop and sniff me as I pass, losing interest when they realise I'm more like them than one of the living.

Finally I come to the block of flats where I grew up. I can see from here that our front door is open. We have electricity in this area but no lights are on inside. It doesn't look like anyone's home. Which is a good thing. My greatest fear as I drew closer was that I'd find Mum, eyes glassed over, human flesh stuck between her teeth, lost to me forever in a state worse than death. (I'm not so worried about Dad, as I'm pretty certain he made it out alive. He has the luck of the devil.) I'm not sure what I'd do if I found her and she was a zombie. I'd want to kill her, to end her suffering, but I don't think that I could.

I spot a few familiar faces on the street, neighbours from a past that seems a thousand years removed. Nobody that I really cared about though. Ignoring them, I crawl up the three flights of stairs – as I pass a giant arse which was spray-painted on the wall, I slap it for luck and grin fleetingly at the memory of happier times – and limp along the landing, then step inside what used to be my home and shut the door on the outside world.

The flat smells musty. The heating hasn't been turned on for months and none of the windows are open. Most of the doors are closed – a habit of Mum's, she couldn't bear an open door – so the rooms are stuffy.

I do a tour of the flat, making sure I'm alone. No blood-stains anywhere, which is a promising sign. No zombies lying in any dark corners either, which is even better. Maybe Mum made it out after all. Perhaps Dad came for her after I split from him at school, took her somewhere safe. They could be living the high life on some paradise island now.

'Yeah,' I sneer at myself. 'Dream on!'

I get a pang in my chest where my heart should be when I look into their bedroom. Some of Mum's clothes are laid across the bed, three different sets. She was obviously choosing what to wear that night when the world went to hell. I can picture her standing here, staring at the clothes, trying to decide. Then ...

What? Killed by a zombie? Turned into one of the living dead? Taken off to some mystical Shangri-La by her racist, wife-beating knight in shining armour?

I don't know. All I know for sure is that she never made a final choice. The clothes stayed here, strewn across the bed, never to be worn again.

'I miss you, Mum,' I moan and wait for tears to come. But of course they don't. They can't. So in the end I close the door and go to check my own room.

It looks smaller than I remembered, dark and poky. I turn on the light, but that just makes it seem even more claustrophobic, full of ominous shadows. I gaze round. My bed looks the same as it always did, crumpled black sheets, the indent of my head on the pillow. No bookshelves or posters. I didn't believe in cluttering up my room. I liked my space, me.

49

I spot my iPod lying on the table next to my bed. I pick it up and smile softly. I left it charging the morning I set off to school for the last time, so it's warm to the touch. I scroll through a couple of my playlists, select a song at random and stick my headphones on. I yelp and immediately turn down the volume. It's easy to forget how good my sense of hearing is. Back then I used to set the volume up almost to maximum. If I did that now, I'd deafen myself.

I let the song play to its end, then lay down the iPod and step out of the room. I'd been looking forward to settling in here again, lying on my old bed and staring at the patch of ceiling which I knew so well. But now that I've seen it, I've gone off the idea. Instead I head back to Mum and Dad's room, sweep the clothes from the bed (I never was overly sentimental), lie back and cross my legs.

'Night night,' I murmur after a few minutes, then turn on my side. I can't sleep, not since I was killed, but there's no harm in pretending every once in a while, is there?

NINE

I spend several days in the flat, maybe even a couple of weeks. Hard to tell for sure — one monotonous day blends into another and I lose track after a while. I only leave three times, to feed. On each occasion, being new to the whole brain-eating game, I track other zombies. They shuffle around the streets, sniffing like pigs in search of truffles. Often they go for hours without finding anything, but in the end they usually manage to track down an old corpse with some scraps of brain still left in its head.

I expected the zombies to fight over the meagre morsels, but they feed politely, taking turns, waiting patiently while others gorge themselves. Sometimes they get a bit overeager and try to butt in, but always pull back if the feasting creature growls warningly at them.

I hate having to feed on the dried-up, rubbery bits of brain, but it's eat or lose my mental faculties completely. I keep looking for animals, but I still haven't seen any, apart from the birds and rats. I've eaten the brains of a few dead crows and rodents, and even caught a live rat once — I think it must have been sick or lame, because it couldn't run very fast. But they haven't made any real difference. Too small. I'd need to tuck into a dog or cat's brain to find out if it could do the job that a human's does for me.

The rest of the time I hole up in the flat, recovering. My wounds don't heal, but the dull ache fades from my bones and my thick, jelly-like blood combines with the green moss to form thin, wispy scabs around the scrapes. After a few days, I'm good as new (well, as close to it as a zombie can ever be), but I make no move to leave. I can't think of anywhere better to go.

I turned on the lights the first night, when I got tired of lying on the bed, but they attracted curious zombies, so I've sat in the dark since then. A few zombies wander in every so often – I've left the front door open, since one of them nearly broke it down when it heard someone at home and couldn't get in – but they slip out once they've satisfied themselves that my brain's of no use to them.

I check the TV every day but it produces nothing but static. The radio, on the other hand, is still going strong. I never used to listen to the radio – *so* twentieth century! – but Mum always had it playing in the background when she was cooking, ironing, etc.

There are far less channels than before. One for official state news, which plays all the time, run by whatever remains of our government and civil service, plus a few independents which broadcast sporadically.

The state reporters give the impression that the military have everything in hand, that they're restoring order, people shouldn't panic, it's all going to work out fine. The independents give more of a sense of the chaos that the world is experiencing. Some of them are critical of the soldiers, claiming they've been opening fire wildly in certain areas, killing the living as well as the dead. A few drop dark hints that the military staged the zombie coup and are eliminating anyone they don't approve of.

I don't pay too much attention to the politics of specific broadcasters. I'm not interested in any particular pundit's opinion. I just want to get to grips with as many cold, hard facts as I can. By switching between the various channels, and filtering out the positive spin of the state channel and the manic gloom of the independents, I fill in a lot of the blanks and get up to speed with what's been going on in the world since my heart was ripped out all those months ago.

Zombies launched simultaneous attacks in most major cities. New York, Tokyo, Moscow, Sydney, Berlin, Johannesburg and scores more, torn apart by the living dead, ruined graveyards of the grand cities they used to be.

The undead spread swiftly. They were almost impossible

to stop. Armies everywhere opposed them, but all it needed was for one zombie to infect a couple of soldiers, and soon they were fighting among themselves, forced to break ranks and retreat. Estimates of the numbers lost to the hordes of the walking dead vary wildly, but most reporters agree that it's probably somewhere between four and five billion.

I have to repeat that slowly to myself the first time I hear it, and even then I can't really comprehend it. Four or five *billion*, most of the world's population, slaughtered or reduced to the status of reanimated corpses. How's this planet ever supposed to recover from that?

Nobody knows where the zombies came from, how the disease manifested itself so swiftly, so globally. And, in truth, nobody's overly concerned. Right now their first priority is survival.

When the attacks started, many small islands were spared. Survivors flocked to those on planes and boats. At first the residents accepted everyone. But then a few islands fell when boats docked or planes set down and zombies streamed out of them, having sneaked aboard. After that, the locals in other places began implementing security checks and setting up quarantine zones, opening fire on anyone who tried to bypass the process.

On the mainland continents, millions of people who can't get to the islands have established fortresses wherever they can. In some cases they've barricaded themselves into apartment complexes, prisons, schools or shopping malls.

Even though their forces have been severely depleted, the armies of the world are the sole governors of society now. Most politicians were wiped out in the first wave of attacks, and those who survived no longer have any real clout. It's martial law wherever you turn.

The troops in the UK have been busy reclaiming lost ground from the zombies. They've converted a series of towns and villages across the country into fortified barracks, building huge walls around them, including areas of open fields within the fortifications so that they can cultivate the land and live off what they grow.

The reporters on the state channel are proud of the army's sterling work and every news bulletin includes reports from some of the reclaimed towns, focusing on the resilience of the people living and working there, their struggle to survive, the way they're doing all that they can to rebuild normal lives for themselves.

The independents are more scathing. They say that residents are treated like cattle, forced to do whatever the soldiers tell them. If they resist, aerial units are sent to blow holes in their defences, to let zombies stream through freely.

I'm not convinced by the wilder reports, but in this zombie-plagued new world, who knows for sure? I keep an open mind, filing everything away.

The army's ultimate aim is to push the zombies back, section them off, then wipe them out. But that will take time. At the moment they're not equipped to engage in a full-on war with the undead. As stern generals keep explaining, their current focus must be on the three Rs — Reclaim, Recruit, Recover. Reclaim towns, recruit more survivors, recover their strength. *Then* they can let rip.

It's terrifying at first, thinking of humanity reduced to this, living off scraps, penned into grimy hovels, under constant siege by their former colleagues and relatives, knowing that all it takes is a single breach – one lone zombie in the mix – for everything they've worked so hard for to come crashing down around them.

But after a while, I get used to it. This is the norm now. You can only be shocked by a thing for so long before it starts to lose its impact. Yeah, the world's a dark, terrible place, and it's horrible listening to stories of children eating their parents or mothers chowing down on their young. But, y'know, when all's said and done, you've got to get on with things.

I only keep following the news after the first few days because of one particular story. The army has been making rescue attempts recently. Lots of people are trapped in cities, even after so many months, lying low at night, foraging for food and drink in the daytime while the zombies are at rest.

The military announce a city a few days ahead of a

planned mission, telling the people who are listening to get ready. Then, on the morning of the rescue, they declare a meeting point and fly in at an appointed time, usually the middle of the day when the sun is at its strongest. They aren't always able to rescue everyone who turns up, and sometimes zombies attack, cutting the evacuation short. But they've extracted hundreds of refugees and escorted them to secure settlements, and have vowed to carry on.

Things would be a lot easier if the phones worked, but as I found out early on when I tested ours, they're even deader than the zombies. All of the landlines are down and all of the mobile networks too. The internet is screwed as well. The only way the army can contact trapped survivors is through the news on the radio, but that's a one-way means of communication.

According to the reports, there have been a few rescues in London already. As the capital, it's been granted priority status. They did trial runs in some of the smaller cities first, but now they're hitting London regularly, a different part every time, so as to keep one step ahead of the zombies.

The walking dead aren't as senseless as they appear. They seem to remember lots of functions, such as how to open doors or operate lifts. They've adapted — if they see a car passing a certain spot at a certain time more than once, they can anticipate its reappearance and lie in wait for it.

But they don't seem to understand most of what is said to

them. They react to certain tones of voice, recognising a variety of commands, the way a baby or a dog can. But they're not able to listen to a broadcast and pitch up at a scheduled meeting place in advance.

If the living are to win this war, it will only be because they can out-think their opponents. In every other respect the zombies are a superior force, far greater in number, able to fight without tiring, not needing food or drink to continue. They don't have any weapons, but their bodies are deadly enough, diseased missiles that are much more effective than a bomb dropped in the middle of a confined group of people.

There have been two missions to London while I've been listening, one in the north, one in the west. Both pick-up points were out of my way, so I stayed put and let them pass. But it's only a matter of time before they come to the East End or the City, and I'm determined to go along when a rescue is announced.

There have been no reports of revitaliseds on any of the radio programmes. The world doesn't seem to be aware of the existence of zombies like me. I'm not sure how the soldiers will react when I turn up, but I've got to try to tell them about the possible threat which revitaliseds pose.

I've been thinking about Rage a lot, the way he killed Dr Cerveris, his contempt for the living. If he survived and made it out of the complex, maybe he looks upon the zombies as his allies. It might amuse him to betray humanity. Perhaps there are others like him who've been mistreated by the living, wanting to get revenge and see them brought low.

I don't know if the soldiers will give me a chance to explain, if they'll offer me shelter in return for my help or shoot me the instant they set eyes on me. I suspect it might be the latter. But I've got to at least try to help, because I was one of the living once, and if I don't cling to that memory and honour it, all that's left for me is the monstrous, lonely, sub-existence of the dead.

TEN

The call finally comes late one evening. There's going to be a mission to Central London in three days — to make it clear, the reporter says that today is Sunday and the rescue will take place sometime on Wednesday. She's excited when she breaks the news. The other rescues in the capital have all been in the suburbs. This is the first time they've hit the centre. They think it might be the largest operation yet, so they're going to be sending more helicopters and troops than normal. But she tells people not to worry, this is just the first mission of many, so if you can't make it this time, stay low and wait for the next.

I head off first thing in the morning. It won't take me three days to walk to the West End, but I want to allow myself plenty of time to overcome any unexpected obstacles along the way, explore the area, find a resting place, maybe meet up with some of the survivors and convince them of my good intentions so that they can act as middlemen between me and the soldiers.

I pause in the doorway of the flat and glance back one last time, nostalgic, remembering Mum and Dad, the bad times as well as the good. And, being honest, there were more bad days than good. Dad was always too free with his fists. Mum and I were constantly walking on eggshells, afraid we'd say the wrong thing and set him off.

But you know what? I'd take them all back in an instant if they were offered, even the days when he beat us and drew blood and kicked us like dogs. He was a nasty sod, there's no denying that, but he was still my dad. I love him. I miss him. I can't help myself.

'I'll come looking for you,' I say aloud to the memories of the two people who mattered to me most. 'If I survive, and you're out there, I'll try to find you, to let you know I made it through, to help you if I can.'

There's no answer or sign that somewhere, somehow, they magically heard. Of course not. I'd have to be a right dozy cow to believe that they're sitting up in a far-off compound, frowning at the ghostly echo of my voice, whispering with awe, '*B?*'

'You're getting soft, girl,' I mutter, then slam the door shut and head on down the stairs, whistling dreadfully — I can't carry a tune these days, not now that my mouth is drier than a camel's arse.

*

I wind my way through the streets, heading west. I've never walked this stretch of London before. We always got a bus or the Tube if we were going up the West End, or a cab on occasions when Dad was feeling flush.

I replace my clothes and jacket as soon as I can, for full protection from the sun. I'm still wearing the Australian hat. That should last me years if I don't lose it. Well, *would* last me years if I lived that long, but I've probably only got about a year and a half, max. Which means this might well prove to be a lifelong hat.

The streets are quiet. I spot zombies in the shade of shops and houses, or resting in abandoned cars or buses. They stare at me hungrily as I amble past. I always make sure I turn so that they can see the hole in my chest. If it wasn't so bright, they'd probably clamber out to make sure I wasn't trying to fool them, but they're reluctant to brave the glare of the day. They haven't thought of wearing sunglasses. They ain't bright sparks like me.

I'm excited to be on the move, to have a goal, even if it's one that could result in my execution. I never did much when I was alive, just hung out with my mates (most or all of them are probably dead now, but I try not to brood about that) or festered in my room. It wasn't a fascinating life by any standards. But it beat the hell out of being held prisoner underground, and the monotony of the last few weeks. I was going stir-crazy in that flat, but I only realise how bad things were now that I've left. You know you've been seriously climbing the walls if the thought of heading off on a suicide mission makes you feel happy!

I lose my way a couple of times, but don't bother checking the *A to Z*. It's a nice day, I'm enjoying the stroll, no zombies or hunters are hassling me, so what's the rush?

I come to a railway station. Lots of eerie-looking train carriages, windows smashed in many, bloodstains splashed across the metal and glass in more places than I can count. On one carriage I spot a large red z with an arrow underneath, pointing west. It looks like it was freshly sprayed — there's even a smell of paint in the air, or is that my imagination?

I swing a right past the station and follow the road round until I can cut through to Victoria Park. Mum used to bring me for walks up here at the weekend when I was younger. Dad came with us sometimes, but he'd always work himself up into a mood, muttering about all the foreigners on the loose.

He wouldn't mind it now. There's not a soul to be seen, black, brown or any other colour. Lots of corpses and bones but that's all. I've got the entire park to myself.

Well ... not quite. As I pad past the tennis courts and come to a few small ponds, I spot three skinny dogs lapping water from a pool.

I perk up when I clock the dogs and hurry towards them, calling out, 'Hey! Doggies! Here!' I make clicking sounds with my tongue.

The dogs react instantly, but not in the way I'd like. Without even looking at me, they take off, yapping fearfully. I race after them, shouting for them to come back, but they're faster than me and disappear from sight moments later. I come to a stop and swear, then kick the ground with anger.

A little later, walking through the park, I regret swearing. I can't blame the dogs for running. These past months must have been hellish for any animal trapped here. If zombies eat an animal's brain as readily as a human's, they'll have gone for every pet in the city. To survive, you'd have to learn to be sneaky, to only come out in the daytime, to avoid all contact with the two-legged creatures which were once so nice to you. I think even Dr Dolittle would have trouble getting animals to trust him these days.

I spend an hour or more in the park. My skin's itching from the sun, even protected by my heavy layers of clothes, but I press on, determined not to let that spoil the day for me. A pity there's nobody selling ice cream. I could murder a 99, even though I'd have to spit out almost every mouthful because I can't digest solids any more.

I keep hoping the dogs will show again, that they'll realise I mean them no harm, that I only crave their friendship, not their brains — as hungry as I get, I wouldn't kill a dog, any more than I'd kill a living person. I want them to slink forward, give me a closer once-over, learn to trust me. But no such luck. They've gone into hiding and I doubt they'll come here again any time soon.

Eventually I take a road leading west. There are dead zombies hanging from the street lamps, rotting in the sun. Each has been shot through the head. Many have been disembowelled or cut up with knives. Flies buzz around the stinking corpses. I pass them nervously, wondering if this was the work of hunters like Barnes and his posse.

I don't like the way that the corpses have been strung up. As vicious as the living dead are, they're not consciously evil, just slaves to their unnatural desires. I understand the need to kill the undead, but torturing and humiliating them serves no purpose. It's not like other zombies are going to look at them and have a change of heart. Being a zombie isn't a career choice. The reviveds don't have any control over what they do.

I turn left, then right on to Bethnal Green Road. One of Mum's best friends, Mary Byrne, lived around here. Her oldest son, Matt, was my age, and his brother Joe was just a bit younger. We used to play together when our mums hung out.

More zombies are strung up along the road ahead of me, but I'm not paying attention to them, trying to remember exactly where Mary lived. So it's a real shock, as I'm walking along, when one of the corpses kicks out at my head and makes a choked noise.

'Bloody hell!' I yell, falling over and scrabbling away.

The zombie goes on kicking and mewling, and I realise I have nothing to fear. I get to my feet and study the writhing figure. It's a man. He's been stripped bare. His hands are tied behind his back and a noose around his neck connects to the lamp overhead. But the people who strung up the zombies left this one alive, either for sport or because they were scared off before they could finish the job.

The man's flesh is a nasty red colour, where he's been burnt by the sun. His eyes are sickly white orbs. He snarls angrily and kicks out furiously at the world. No telling how long he's been up there, but by the state of his eyes, I'd say it's been a good while.

I should press on but I can't. This guy means nothing to me but I can't leave him like this. I wouldn't do this to anyone, even a savage killer, as he doubtless would become if given his freedom and a human target.

'Hold on, sunshine,' I tell him. 'I'll find a ladder and come free you.'

The zombie screeches hoarsely, limited by the rope around his throat.

'Be patient,' I snap. 'I won't be long. Just give me a few minutes to go search for ...'

66

I come to a stunned halt. I was turning to look for a hardware store when I spotted something, just past the corner where I cut on to this stretch. I do a double take, but when I look again it's still there.

An artist's easel has been set in the middle of the road, straddling a white line. A medium-sized canvas rests on it. And just behind the easel stands a man, holding a painter's palette, gawping at me as if I'd come from another planet.

'Who the bloody hell are you?' I roar, striding towards him.

The man yelps and drops the palette. He turns and runs. I give immediate chase. He's faster than me, but I throw myself through the air, taking long jumps, and a few seconds later I overtake him and draw to a halt, blocking his way. The man screams and turns to run back the way he's come.

'Don't try it!' I shout. 'I don't need to breathe, so I can chase you all day and never drop my pace.'

The man shudders, glances around desperately for a place to hide or something to defend himself with. Finding nothing, he resigns himself, straightens and turns to face me. He brushes dried flecks of paint from the sleeves of his coat and tries a shaky smile.

'My name is Timothy Jackson,' he squeaks, as posh as you like.

'What are you doing here?' I snap.

'Painting.' He nods at the easel and beams proudly,

forgetting for a moment that he should be trembling with fear. 'I'm an artist.'

As I stare at him, lost for words, he mistakes my gaze for one of hunger and loses his confidence as quickly as he found it. With a gulp, his arms slump by his sides and he says in a low, miserable voice, 'Please don't eat me.'

ELEVEN

I circle the artist warily as he stands shivering and wincing. He's not very old, maybe early thirties. Medium height, a bit on the thin side, with a long face and dark circles round his eyes. He's wearing yellow trousers, a pink shirt and a tweed jacket. His clothes are dirty, ruined with paint, but look like they came from a top-notch shop. He has long, untidy brown hair, but is freshly shaven, not even a hint of stubble. He stinks of strong aftershave, like he bathes in the stuff.

I squint at the canvas on which he was working. It depicts the zombie hanging from the rope. The feet look too big, out of proportion to the rest of the body, but I suspect that's deliberate.

'Did you stick him up there?' I growl.

Timothy laughs nervously. 'Hardly. I found him here a few days ago and I've been coming back to paint him at different times of the day, to take advantage of the changing light.'

'He's suffering. Zombies can't endure the sun. He's burnt and going blind. You never thought about letting him down?'

Timothy blinks and scratches his head. 'To be honest, no, I didn't. It's not that I derive any pleasure from his pain – I feel sorry for these poor creatures – but if I'd set him free, he would have come after me and either gouged out my brain or turned me into a monster like him.'

I have to acknowledge that he's got a point.

'I'll let you off this time,' I sniff.

'If it's not impudent of me,' Timothy murmurs, eyes round and filled with curiosity, 'what on earth *are* you? I thought you were one of the undead when I first saw you, but then you spoke.'

'I'm a revitalised,' I tell him. 'A zombie who regained its thoughts.'

'That's possible?' he gasps.

'In some cases, yeah.'

'Does that mean there's a cure for the rest of them?'

I shrug. 'I don't think so.'

Although, now that I consider it, maybe it does. Perhaps a serum could be fashioned from my blood, one that could restore thought to all of the living dead. If I get rescued on Wednesday, I'll suggest that to the soldiers. I don't mind being a guinea pig, not if I can help bring peace to the world.

Hell, maybe I'll end up being hailed as a hero. B Smith —
saviour of mankind!

'Enough about me,' I grunt. 'What the hell is an artist
doing in the middle of the road in a city overrun by zombies?'

'Capturing the apocalypse for the sake of posterity,'
he beams. 'I've been doing this every day since London
fell. Well, not for the first couple of weeks – it was too dangerous to venture out – but I've not missed a day since.'

'And you haven't been attacked in all that time?' I ask
sceptically.

'Of course I have,' he chuckles. 'I've had to race for my
life more times than I can count. There are tricks I've learnt
to employ which help ward off interest – I don't come out if
it's cloudy, I douse myself in strong cologne to mask my
scent, I make as little noise as possible – but I get spotted
and chased two or three times a day on average.'

I frown. 'How come you haven't been caught yet?'

'A healthy mix of skill and luck,' he says, then pauses. 'Do
you have a name?'

'Of course. I'm B Smith.'

'And you're not going to eat me, are you, B?'

'Nah. You don't look that tasty,' I laugh.

'You won't snap suddenly, lose your mind and turn on
me?' he presses.

'No.'

71

'You're a good zombie?'

I smile. 'I probably wouldn't go that far. But I'm not a killer.'

Timothy mulls that over, then nods to himself. 'In that case, do you mind if we head back to my place? I don't like talking out here in the open. Sounds carry and zombies have a keen sense of hearing.'

'Where do you live?' I ask.

'Close by. I never venture too far from my studio. Come, we can chat on the way, and I'd love to show you my work. Are you interested in art at all?'

'Not really,' I mutter and his face falls. 'But if it's drawings of zombies and the city, I definitely want to have a look.'

Timothy's smile returns full force. 'Excellent!' Picking up his easel and palette, he heads down Bethnal Green Road, whistling jauntily, strutting like a peacock.

TWELVE

Timothy looks like a man without a care in the world, but I note the way he casts careful glances at the buildings on either side, keeping an eye out for zombies. He's not as reckless as he appears, although his very presence here proves that he's something of a daredevil.

He comes to the turn for Brick Lane and pauses. 'That's where we're headed,' he says, nodding at the street which used to contain London's most famous string of curry houses.

'We're not going for an Indian, are we?' I joke.

'Actually I've made use of the restaurants quite a lot,' he says seriously. 'I ran out of fresh food long ago, but the freezers are still working in many places. I can rustle you up an amazing chicken madras if you're hungry.'

'I'm a zombie,' I remind him. 'I only eat brains.'

He considers that. 'If you supplied the brains, I could

probably do something with them. Mix them up in a korma perhaps.'

I burst out laughing. 'Anyone ever tell you you're a nutjob, Jackson?'

'Only Mother, Father, my teachers and friends.' He sighs. 'But they're all dead or eaten now, so I guess I had the last laugh. All joking aside, I love to cook, so if you want ...'

'Thanks for the offer, but cooking might rob the brains of the nutrients I need. As far as I know, they have to be raw.'

That's nonsense, but it satisfies Timothy and spares me the job of telling him I'd rather eat straight from a corpse's head than risk one of his dishes.

Timothy starts walking again but doesn't turn into Brick Lane.

'I thought you said we were going that way.'

'We are,' he nods, 'but my studio is about halfway down. It's a narrow, dark street. I've boarded up most of the buildings close to mine, but zombies could be lurking somewhere along the way. I always go down the main road and cut in from there. You have to be careful if you want to survive around here.'

At the end of Bethnal Green Road we cut left on to Commercial Street.

'I adored the markets around here,' Timothy says. 'I often came over on a Sunday and spent the entire day milling around, sketching people, buying things I didn't need, sampling the many local varieties of fine cuisine.'

'Fine cuisine?' I snort. 'Bagels and curry?'

'Oh, there was much more than that,' Timothy insists. 'Pies and falafel and jellied eels for instance.'

'*You* ate jellied eels?'

'Why shouldn't I?' he blinks.

'I didn't have you pegged for the jellied eels sort. My gran loved them, and my dad and his mates tucked into them sometimes, but I mean, come on, they were disgusting. Cold, bony bits of eel wrapped up in slimy jelly — you wouldn't feed that mess to a dog.'

'It was authentic East London,' Timothy protests.

'*I'm* authentic East London,' I tell him, 'and I wouldn't touch jellied eels with a bargepole.'

'Well, to each their own,' he says with a shrug.

We turn into a street lined with beautiful old houses. It feeds into Brick Lane and we come to a huge building, the old Truman Brewery. Timothy looks around to make sure no one – no *thing* – is watching, then fishes a key out of a pocket and hurries to a large, steel door. He opens it quickly and slips inside. I get an uneasy feeling – maybe this is a trap and I'm not the first revitalised he's lured back – but then I recall his yellow trousers and chuckle weakly. What sort of a bad guy would wear yellow pants?

Maybe it's just because I'm lonely, but I decide to trust my new-found friend. Putting my doubts behind me, I step into the gloom of the building and try not to show any signs of unease as Timothy gently swings the oversized door shut and cuts us off from the outside world.

THIRTEEN

Timothy throws a switch and lights flicker on all over the place. We're in a spacious room, the sort you might find in a warehouse. The windows have all been boarded over to keep in the light and keep out the zombies.

'Most of that was done before I came,' Timothy says, nodding at the planks nailed over the glass. 'There were five other people sheltering here then, including a security guard who was on duty when the zombies attacked.'

'What happened to them?' I ask.

'Two were captured by zombies over the following weeks. The others decided to make a break for freedom. The last I saw of them, they were heading for the river to search for a boat.'

'Why didn't you go with them?'

He looks at me as if I'm crazy. 'I told you, I'm a painter. I stayed behind to paint.'

Timothy leads me up a short set of stairs and into an even larger room. There are canvases everywhere, most of them blank, along with brushes, tins of paint, easels and all sorts of artistic bits and bobs.

'I loved the East End art scene,' Timothy says as we stride through the room. 'It felt natural that I come here once London fell. I originally meant to make camp in an ordinary house, but when I strolled up Brick Lane and realised this amazing space was occupied by humans and secure, I knew it was fate.'

We climb another set of stairs and come to a massive room. The windows have been boarded over here too, though some cracks have been left between the planks to let light through.

'Why the boards?' I ask. 'Surely you don't need them this high up.'

Timothy squints at me. 'Are you *sure* you're a zombie?'

I point to the hole in my chest.

'Good answer. But then why do you know so little about your kind?'

'I was locked up,' I tell him. 'I only broke free a few weeks ago and I've laid low most nights since then.'

'Well,' Timothy chuckles, 'the good news is that if you like climbing, you're in for a treat. Those bones sticking out of your fingers are extraordinarily durable. They'll dig into wood, brick, all sorts of substances. Determined zombies can scale the walls of old buildings like this.'

The room is crammed with canvases, but unlike those downstairs, these have been worked on. A few are hanging, but most stand on the floor, propped against the walls. In some places they're stacked twelve deep.

'When I first moved in, I thought I'd have all the space I'd ever need,' Timothy says as we slowly circle the room, studying the paintings. 'But I didn't anticipate my muse calling to me so strongly. As you can see, I've been prolific.'

The paintings are dark, ominous, creepy, full of zombies, corpses, deserted streets, spooky sunsets. Even though I'm no art expert, they instantly give me a sense of pain, suffering and loss. It's like stepping into a gallery of Hell.

'Do you like them?' Timothy asks, chewing a nail, trying to act as if he doesn't care about my answer.

'They're unbelievable,' I sigh and his face lights up.

'They *are* rather good, aren't they?' he chirps, picking up one of the canvases and beaming at it. It's a painting of a young girl, her head cracked open, brains spilling on to the pavement, face smeared with blood. But the way he gazes at it, it could be a painting of a bunch of flowers.

'To be honest, I was never the most skilled of artists,' Timothy admits. 'But then the zombies rose up, everyone fled or was killed, I was left here virtually alone, and something changed. It was like I woke up one morning with a new gift.'

Timothy sets down the painting and moves on, looking at

the canvases in much the same way that a zombie looks at human skulls.

'We're living in tragic, terrible times. I believe that I've been spared and given extra talent so that I can document the troubles. A higher force guides me, empowers me, protects me when I'm on the streets. I shouldn't have survived this long. The fact that I have . . .'

He falls silent and stares at the dark paintings. I can see that they mean everything to him.

'Do you believe in God?' Timothy asks me.

I shuffle uneasily. 'I dunno. I don't *not* believe, but I'm not sure.'

'I used to be uncertain too,' he says, then waves an arm around at the atrocities captured on the canvases. 'But who else could have done this to the world? Only the Almighty could have judged mankind and razed it to the ground in such brute, total fashion.

'I don't know why a loving God would do this to us,' he whispers. 'But if I keep on painting, and study that which I've created for long enough, I think I can find out.'

He steps up to one of the paintings, carefully lays his fingers on it and says softly, 'This isn't really the work of Timothy Jackson. These were fashioned by the hand of *God*.'

FOURTEEN

I think Timothy's a nutter, but I say nothing. If he wants to believe that God is working through him, I don't mind. As long as he doesn't try to convert me, he can believe whatever the hell he likes.

Timothy shows me round the rest of the building. His sleeping quarters are basic, just blankets and pillows laid on the floor in one corner of a small room. He has a larder full of canned goods and bottles of water, some wine and champagne too. Several small freezers full of bread, meat and other perishables.

He keeps a radio, but only turns it on once or twice a week to catch up with any major breaking news.

'My greatest worry is that they'll bomb London,' he says. 'There was talk of it in the early days. Zombies are everywhere, but they're especially prevalent in the big cities. According to some reporters, the army chiefs discussed levelling the likes of London and New York. Wiser heads prevailed, but if the rumours are to be believed, the suggestion is still on the table. If they ever go ahead with that, I want to get my paintings out of here. I don't mind if I get blown to pieces, but if the world lost my work, it would be an absolute tragedy.'

As impressive as the paintings are, I don't think their loss could be classed as a global disaster. But I don't share that opinion with Timothy.

'Don't you get lonely?' I ask as we sit in the main room and Timothy tucks into a corned beef sandwich.

'Why should I?' he counters, nodding at the paintings. 'I have those for company. I work all the time when I'm awake and I only sleep for five, maybe six, hours at night. Although I must admit I've often felt exposed. It's dangerous for me out there on the streets, no one to help if I run into trouble. Maybe that's why you've been sent to me.'

'What do you mean?' I frown.

He smiles crookedly. 'I don't think we met by coincidence. It was fate. God wants you to become my bodyguard, to ensure my work can continue.'

As I stare at him, his smile widens. 'You can stay with me. I'll share all that I have, help you find brains, be company for you. We'll be a team, Jackson and Smith, doing the work of the Lord. Neither one of us need ever be alone again.'

That sounds both tempting and creepy at the same time.

'Did you have a partner before all this?' I ask, to change the subject.

He nods, his smile fading. 'Alan. He was a sculptor. He could create the most lifelike hands.'

'What happened to him?'

'He became one of *them*,' Timothy says emotionlessly. 'I went looking for him in his studio, but he'd already been infected. He chased me. Almost killed me. I had to fight for my life. I managed to drive one of his chisels through his head.'

Timothy lays down his sandwich and stares ahead at nothing.

'That was when I created my first painting,' he says softly. 'I mixed Alan's blood with the paint, careful to don gloves before touching it. I painted him as he was, lying there, teeth bared in a death snarl, the handle of the chisel sticking out of his skull. I wept as I painted, knowing it was beautiful, yet hating it at the same time. Part of me – the part that loves, cherishes, cares – died that day. It was a part that needed to die. It would have got in the way of my work.'

He lapses into silence, his expression distant.

'Do you still have that painting?' I ask.

'No. I burnt it and scattered the ashes over Alan's corpse. It would have felt like theft if I'd taken it. That moment belonged to him. I didn't want to steal it.'

'But you've stolen all of these,' I murmur, waving at the canvases.

'Yes,' he sighs. 'I should feel guilty but I don't. I can't afford guilt or love or anything pure like that. To do my job, I have to be as passionless as the zombies I paint and run from.' He smiles fleetingly. 'That might be another reason why I've made it as far as I have. Maybe they realise, as they draw closer, that I'm not so different to them. In many ways I'm one of the walking dead as well ...'

Later Timothy asks if he can sketch me before he hits the sack. I sit for him patiently while he stares at the hole in my chest and tries to bring it to life on a canvas. He shows it to me when he's done. My face is dimly painted with a mix of dark grey colours. All the focus is on the red and green mess around the hole where my boob should be. I hate the way I look in the drawing.

'You don't like it,' Timothy notes, disappointed.

'It's just ... am I really that ugly?' I ask.

He shakes his head. 'You're not ugly at all. But you're a walking corpse. I have to show that, otherwise it won't ring true.'

'That's how I look to you?' I sniff. 'Pale, distant, vicious?'

'Not vicious,' Timothy corrects me. 'I would have said *hungry*. Not just for brains, but for your old life, a cure, the ability to be human again. You hunger for things you can no longer have, and that hunger brings you pain.'

I think about that hours later, while Timothy sleeps. I've stayed in the room of paintings, studying them silently, looking for familiar faces. I *am* in pain, all the time, and it's not just because I'm undead. I lost my parents and friends — whether they're dead, alive or somewhere between, I'll almost certainly never see them again. I threw an innocent boy to a pack of zombies. I killed humans when I turned. I failed to save Mark from the zom heads. I have blood on my hands. There's rot in my soul.

By rights, I should huddle up in a ball and howl, beg for pity, forgiveness, release. I should hurl myself off a tall building or find a gun and blow my brains out. In this cruel world, I can only experience more pain, ruin more lives, kill or infect. If Timothy stumbled when he was painting me, and I reached out to steady him, and one of my nails nicked his flesh . . .

I stare at the monsters in the paintings. I'm no less monstrous than any of them. Maybe I'm worse, still being able to think. They have no choice in what they do, but I have. I could eliminate myself, make sure nobody ever suffered again at my twisted, wretched hands.

But I keep thinking about the possibility of revitalising the rest of the undead hordes. If my blood could be used to restore consciousness in other zombies, it might help bring order back to this crazy, lethal world.

In the morning, when Timothy awakes, I tell him I have to go.

'You're leaving?' He blinks sleepily. 'Did I say something to offend you?'

'No,' I smile. 'But I can't stay. There's going to be a rescue mission soon. I have to surrender, let the soldiers know I'm different, so their scientists can study me and maybe find a way to help other zombies think clearly.'

Timothy hums. 'The soldiers would, I imagine, be more inclined to execute you on sight.'

'Yeah, I know. But I have to try. You can come along too if you want.'

He smiles shyly. 'I can't leave. I belong here. I wish you luck, B, but your way isn't mine. If they reject you, please bear in mind that you will always be welcome in my studio.'

'Thanks.' I chuckle drily. 'I'd like to shake your hand, but ...'

He chuckles too. 'One tiny scratch and I'd be history.'

'If I do get out,' I say hesitantly, 'is there anything you need, anything I can send back to you?'

He shakes his head. 'Just tell people about my work.' He gestures to the canvases. 'We'll all be here, the dead and I, waiting for the world to find us.'

'What if they don't want to find you?' I ask. 'People might not want to look at paintings of zombies, having seen so many of them in the flesh.'

'They will,' he insists. He walks over to the nearest painting, picks it up and gazes into the face of a monster. 'This is the truth, who we are and where we've come from. People are always drawn to the truth. It demands that we acknowledge it and learn.'

He closes his eyes and his face whitens.

'In the end, stripped bare of everything else, as everyone is eventually, all we're left with is the truth.'

I don't understand that, so I leave Timothy hugging his painting, eyes shut, lost to a world of madness or truth or whatever you want to call it.

FIFTEEN

I've loads of time on my hands, so I decide to do a bit of sightseeing as I'm making my way towards the centre of the city, and cut south towards the river.

I come to the Tower of London and stroll around the moat to the main entrance. Amazingly, I've never visited here before, not even on a school tour.

As I approach the gate, I spot a Beefeater standing in the shadows of a hut. He growls and steps forward, squinting in the light. Part of his throat has been bitten out and green moss grows round the hole like a wayward beard. I let him examine the gap in my chest. Once he's had a good look, I start forward, but he stops me.

'Out of my way,' I snap, but when I try to wriggle past, he pushes me back. 'I'm one of you, idiot!' I shout, and shove him aside.

The Beefeater slams an elbow into the side of my head as

I'm passing, catching me by surprise. I haven't seen any zombies fighting with one another. I didn't think I had anything to fear. Seems like I should have been more cautious.

As I stagger around, the inside of my skull ringing wildly, the Beefeater grabs me and hauls me to the ground. He pins me with his knees and makes a howling, gurgling sound before baring his teeth and leaning forward to chew through my skull.

I thought I'd be able to outsmart a zombie in a one-on-one struggle, but the Beefeater has me bang to rights. All I can do is stare at him with horror as he opens his mouth wide and presses his fangs to the cold flesh of my forehead.

For a few seconds the Beefeater holds that position. My sights are locked on the hole in his throat. If I could get a hand free, I could maybe rip the hole wide open. As I'm considering that, and wondering why the Beefeater has paused, he leans back and looks at me stiffly. To my astonishment he holds up a hand and makes a pinching gesture with his thumb and fingers. Then he cocks his head sideways, questioningly.

'You've got to be kidding,' I groan, realising what the issue is.

The Beefeater snarls and makes the gesture with his fingers again. He's a mindless, cannibalistic killer, but somewhere deep in that ruined brain of his, an old spark of instinct is driving him to do what he did every working day when he was alive.

'OK,' I wheeze. 'If you let me up, I'll play ball. I'm a good girl, I am.'

The Beefeater squints at me. I offer a shaky smile. He grunts and gets off, studying me suspiciously, as if he thinks I'm going to try and trick him.

Shaking my head with disbelief, I get to my feet and make for the ticket office which I passed on my way. The windows have been smashed in. I lean over the counter and grab a ticket from the nearest machine. Returning to the gate, I hand the ticket to the jobsworth of a zombie Beefeater. He takes it from me, nods gruffly and returns to his post, letting me through.

Unbe-bloody-lievable!

I go on a tour of the famous buildings, but most are packed with zombies – including a lot of overweight tourists who probably prefer their brains in batter and deep-fried – so I stick to the paths for the most part. I'm sorry I didn't come when it was operational. I couldn't care less about the Crown jewels, but I'd have loved to learn more about the prisoners who were held here and all the heads that were chopped off.

I recall the legend that if the ravens ever fled the Tower or died out, the city would fall. I always dismissed that as a story most likely cooked up by a raven-handler who wanted to make sure he was never driven out of a job. But as I wander, I note glumly that there isn't a bird to be seen, apart from a few brittle bones, beaks and feathers.

Coincidence? Probably. But it gives me a mild dose of the creeps all the same. Did some scraggly, wild-eyed soothsayer predict this disaster all those centuries ago? Was this plague of the living dead always destined to happen? Uneasy, I push on sooner than I'd meant to, waving goodbye to the Beefeater as I pass, no hard feelings. In an odd sort of way I respect him. He's stuck true to his principles, even in death. I don't mind that he roughed me up. In his position I like to think that I'd do the same.

I cross Tower Bridge. It hasn't escaped the turmoil unscathed. A plane came down in this area – I guess a zombie must have got onboard and caused chaos – and chunks of the wreckage are lying in the river where it crashed. On its way, it took out the two walkways at the top of the bridge, smashing straight through them. The towers that they were attached to weren't damaged. It's as if someone came along and snipped off the connecting tunnels with a giant pair of scissors.

Rubble from the walkways is strewn across the road and footpaths, so I have to zigzag my way across. I pause at the point where the two halves of the bridge meet. How cool would it be if I found the engine rooms and raised the drawbridge!

I grin as I imagine it, then shake my head regretfully. Time might be on my side, but I don't have *that* much to play with. Besides, I'm not a child. I'm on a deadly serious mission. This is proper, grown-up business.

The strangely-shaped, glass-fronted mayor's building is gleaming in the sun, half-blinding me. I hurry on past and head for HMS *Belfast*, thinking I might go for a stroll around the deck. But as I approach, I spot humans onboard. They've barricaded the gangway and several are standing guard, heavy rifles hanging by their sides. As I stare at the living people, bewildered to find them here, one of them spots me, raises his gun and opens fire.

Yelping, I duck out of sight and wait for the bullets to stop. When they do, I take off my jacket and wave it at the people on the boat.

'Ahoy!' I roar, getting all nautical. 'My name's B Smith. I don't mean you any harm. I want to –'

The guy starts shooting again before I can finish. Bullets rip through my jacket and one almost blows a couple of my fingers off. Cursing, I drop the jacket, then yank it to safety. I don't know who the people on the boat are, but they clearly like their own company, and when someone's armed to the teeth and quick on the trigger, a wise girl gives them all the space in the world that they want.

I detour via Tooley Street. I remember Dad telling me that the London Dungeon used to be here before it moved. I always loved that ghoulish maze of torment and atrocity, but I don't think I'll ever bother with it again. This city of the dead boasts more than enough public horrors, like the hanging zombie on . . .

I stop and wince — the zombie who was dangling from the lamp post on Bethnal Green Road! I meant to free him when I left Timothy's place, but I forgot all about him. It's no biggie. In fact it seems ridiculous to worry about a single zombie in this city of monsters. But if I was in his position and someone had the power to set me free and didn't . . .

What if you free him and he ends up killing Timothy? part of me sulks as I turn to head back the way I came.

'That's life,' I shrug.

The zombie doesn't thank me when I cut him down, or show the least sign that he's grateful. Instead, having paused to sniff me in case I'm worth tucking into, he hurries away, seeking shelter, stumbling into anything in his path, unable to see clearly out of his almost totally white eyes.

Feeling more of a time-wasting fool than a good Samaritan, I retrace my steps and make it back to Tooley Street by early afternoon. Moving on, I slip past Southwark Bridge and cast a wary eye over the shell of the Globe. I never went to a show there – wild horses couldn't have dragged me – but I know all about this place. It's where they used to put on Shakespearean plays every summer.

As I consider the fact that nobody will ever stage a three- or four-hour version of *Hamlet* or *King Lear* here ever again, I break out into a smile and chuckle wickedly — the downfall of civilisation isn't *all* bad news!

SIXTEEN

I'm heading for the impressive-looking Tate Modern when I spot a small boat pulling up to the pier. I watch with astonishment as nine people pile out and march towards shore like tourists on a day trip.

But these aren't like any tourists I've ever seen. All nine – four men and five women – are dressed in blue robes. Their arms are bare. Each has a tiny blue symbol scrawled across their forehead. And they chant softly as they progress.

I hang back as the group ignores the art museum and heads on to the pedestrian bridge, which my dad used to call the Wobbly Bridge, since it wobbled so badly when it first opened that they had to close it for months to steady it up.

Something about these people unsettles me. They don't seem to be carrying any weapons, yet they're walking around openly. Hasn't anyone told them about the zombies?

I follow the group on to the bridge, wait until we're

halfway across – St Paul's Cathedral towers ahead of us – then call out to them, 'Hey!'

They stop but don't turn. I edge closer, skin prickling, ready to dive over the side of the bridge if they produce guns from beneath their robes and open fire. But although the men and women glance at me as I slip past them, nobody reacts in any other way.

The woman at the head of the group studies me with a solemn expression as I stop before her. She's pretty, but has a pinched, stern face. Her hair is pure white – all the others have white hair too, which makes me think it's dye – so it's hard to judge her age.

'You are one of the restless dead,' the woman says, having noted the hole in my chest.

'Yeah.'

She cocks her head. 'I did not know that the undead could speak.'

'Most can't. I'm an exception.'

The woman nods, then spreads her arms wide. 'I am Sister Clare, of the Order of the Shnax. Have you come to attack us, foul creature of the lost?'

'No.'

'You have not come to slice open our skulls and feast on our brains?' she presses, pale blue eyes hard in the glaring sunlight.

'Not unless you want me to,' I joke.

'There!' the woman exclaims to those behind her. 'The blessings of the Shnax are with us, as I told you they would be.'

The people in the robes mutter appreciatively and bow their heads. Sister Clare basks in their adulation, then trains her gaze on me again.

'Are you a vile imp sent to guide us?' she asks haughtily.

'No,' I growl, resisting the urge to punch her on the nose. 'I saw you getting out of the boat and was curious. I wanted to warn you as well. It's dangerous here. The zombies –'

'We know all about them,' she interrupts. 'They are why we have come, to test our faith against theirs.'

'What are you talking about?' I frown. 'Zombies don't have any faith. They're brainless.'

'They are instruments of the dark forces of the universe,' she corrects me. 'By walking without fear among them, we will challenge those who work through their pitiful forms and reclaim this ground that they would steal from us. If you mean neither to help nor hinder us, then step aside or face the wrath of the Shnax.'

The woman waves a hand at me and glides past imperiously. The others follow, nodding and mumbling. A few smirk at me. One of the men touches the symbol on his forehead, then points at me as if to say, 'I've got my eye on you!'

I don't care much for Sister Clare or her sneering tone, but these weirdos have caught my attention. I can't resist following, to find out what they're up to. So, ignoring the fact that they don't care for my company, I trail after them as they cross the bridge and wander into the zombie-infested bowels of the city.

SEVENTEEN

The fearless members of the Order of the Shnax march to St Paul's and stop outside, chanting happily, beaming at one another. The sun is shining brightly and no zombies are on the streets. It's as if we have the city to ourselves.

Sister Clare leads the group on a full circuit of the cathedral, then heads east. I try to wring more information out of her as they proceed.

'You know you're all going to be killed.'

She raises an eyebrow. 'You might wish for our deaths, vulgar beast of the otherworld, but you will be disappointed. We have the power of the Shnax on our side. No harm will befall us.'

'What *are* the Shnax?' I press. 'Some sort of religious group?'

'We are of the true religion,' Sister Clare tells me and points a finger at the sky. 'The religion of the stars.'

'The stars...' the others echo dreamily, all pointing upwards.

'Celestial beings have always gazed down on us,' Sister Clare continues. 'Since the dawn of mankind they have encouraged us, rewarded us when we are deserving, punished us when we have sinned. They are the Shnax.'

'Aliens?' I laugh. 'Pull the other one!'

She smiles condescendingly. 'Like so many others, you can only mock. That is why you were turned into a pitiful mockery of the human form while we were spared. This world was disgusting, overcrowded with vain, petty humans. It needed clearing so that a fresh, clean civilisation could grow out of the ashes of the old.

'The Shnax would never have done this to us, since they are creatures of love, but there are other forces at work in the universe, agents of destruction. The Shnax protected us from them in the past, but this time, for our own good, they let their foes wreak havoc. But they shielded the believers and kept us safe, so that we can guide the others who survived.'

I gawp at Sister Clare and the lunatics who follow her.

'You think that you know better than us,' Sister Clare smirks. 'I see it in your eyes, as lifeless as they are.'

'Come on,' I chuckle uneasily. 'You can't really believe that aliens did this or that they're guarding you.'

'If not the Shnax, then who?' she asks.

'The government ... scientists ... terrorists ... take your pick.'

She shakes her head. 'This apocalypse was not the work of humans. No mortal could have subjected the world to terrors on such a diabolic scale. Mankind has been culled. The weak have been cut down and set against the strong. It is the result of a godly hand, but there are no gods meddling in our affairs, only the Shnax.'

'Who told you about these aliens? Did you read about them in a magazine? See a show on TV?'

'They contacted me directly,' she sniffs. 'They spoke to me in dreams to begin with. Later I learnt to put myself into a trance and speak with them that way.'

'So you hear voices,' I murmur.

'Go ahead,' she snaps, her smile vanishing. 'Laugh at me. You won't be the first. But I told people this would happen. Nobody believed me until it was too late. Now that the worst has come to pass, people are starting to see that I was right. These are the first of my disciples, but they will not be the last. When we emerge from these haunted streets, alive and untouched, more will flock to our side. The survivors will see that I am the mouthpiece of the Shnax, and the world will finally offer us the respect which we are due.'

Sister Clare turns to the others and cries, 'Out of the darkness of the skies came the Shnax!'

'Out of the darkness!' they respond, heads bobbing, fingers twitching.

The fanatics carry on, wandering aimlessly. I think about

abandoning them – I should be heading west, not wasting my time on these maniacs – but I'll feel bad if I leave them without at least trying to make them see sense.

'You can't really believe that aliens will save you from the zombies,' I challenge them.

'How else are we protected?' Sister Clare retorts smugly, waving a hand at the buildings around us. 'These are the homes of the damned, populated by the lost and vicious hordes, yet no monster comes out to attack us.'

'You've been lucky,' I argue. 'Sunlight hurts zombies. They rest up in the daytime. If you're still here when night falls . . .' I draw a finger across my throat.

Sister Clare scowls at me. 'You know nothing of these matters, child of the lost. Leave us be.'

'I know that you're mad,' I snap. 'And I know you don't truly believe what you're preaching. You'd put your lives fully on the line if you did.'

'What are you talking about?' Sister Clare asks, drawing to a halt.

'It's brave of you to come here,' I drawl, smiling tightly at the men and women in the robes. 'But you'd have come when it was dark if you wanted to prove beyond doubt that you were under heavenly protection. Or you'd go into one of these buildings, packed with the living dead, stand in the middle of them and chant away to your heart's content. But you don't because you know deep down that you'd be eaten alive.'

I flash my sharp teeth at them. Sister Clare's face reddens and she opens her mouth to have a go at me. But then one of the men says, 'The girl speaks the truth.'

Sister Clare's eyes fill with rage. 'You doubt me, Sean?' she shrieks.

'No,' the man called Sean says without lowering his gaze. 'I believe. But we must face our enemy. If the Shnax are looking down on us kindly, as I'm sure they are, we can walk through the ranks of the undead and the whole world will know that what we say is true. Otherwise people will sneer at us, as she has, and claim it was merely good fortune that we passed through these streets unharmed.'

Sister Clare licks her lips nervously. I catch a glimpse of uncertainty in her expression. Part of her knows this is madness.

'I can lead you back to your boat,' I say softly. 'You can return to wherever you were hiding before. You'll die if you go on.'

She stares at me for a long moment. Then she spits in my face. As I pull back, shocked, she faces her followers. 'The demon wants to lure us back to our boat and send us on our way. She is afraid of us, afraid of the Shnax.'

The other men and women start jeering and spitting at me. My temper flares and I flex my fingers, ready to rip them to pieces. I take a step forward, snarling. I think, if Sister Clare stepped away, I'd go for her. But she doesn't retreat.

Instead she takes a step towards me, tilting her head back, offering her throat.

'Go ahead, servant of the darkness,' she hisses. 'Kill me if that is what your foul masters demand. I will die happily in the service of the Shnax.'

The others fall to their knees and offer their throats too. I shake my head and lower my hand, remembering Tyler Bayor, recalling my vow to be a better person.

Sister Clare tuts. Then her features soften. 'No, it is wrong of me to blame you for what you have become. You were weak, as so many were, but it is not for us to condemn you. You are suffering enough.'

Her gaze settles on something behind me. She starts to smile again. 'But the imp is right about one thing, brothers and sisters. We *do* need to confront the forces of darkness directly, to prove beyond a shadow of a doubt that we are blessed. Let us face our destiny and show the world that ours is the one true way. Follow me!'

Sister Clare sets off at a jog. The others rise and hurry after her, chanting even faster than before, buzzing now, ready to follow their leader into the jaws of Hell if she demands it of them.

Turning to see where they're going, I realise she's leading them to a place even deadlier than the fabled gates of the underworld. We've come to the threshold of Liverpool Street Station. There are probably scores of zombies down there on the concourse, sheltering from the sun. Sister Clare is at the top of the steps which descend into that murky den of the dead.

'No!' I yell. 'Don't do it. I didn't mean to dare you. I believe. You don't have to prove anything to me. Come back.'

But Sister Clare only flashes me a smile of twisted triumph. Then she heads down, followed by the others, into the zombie-friendly gloom.

EIGHTEEN

I can't bear to let them go off by themselves, so I race after them, down the steps into the stomach of what was once commuter heaven.

It's not as dark down here as I thought. The station lets in quite a lot of light, so most of the zombies in residence have avoided the concourse. Still, there must be a hundred or more of the beasts who were resting in the shade around the main ring of the station. And every single one of them is now pushing forward, closing in on the nine robed, doomed humans.

Sister Clare acts as if she's unaware of the threat and marches to the centre of the concourse. Her chant turns into a song and the others take it up, a dull tune about stars and aliens and how the chosen will be spared the wrath of the skies.

The deluded humans come to a halt in the middle of the

station and form a circle, hands linked, feet planted firmly, singing joyously. The zombies push in closer … closer …

Then stop about a metre away.

I stare with disbelief at the white-haired men and women singing loudly, the zombies massed around them but not moving in for the kill, swaying softly as if held in place by the sound of the song. Or by something else?

It's crazy, but I find myself starting to wonder. As I slip through the ranks of the living dead, into the empty space around Sister Clare and her followers, I'm ready to believe. Why not? Their story makes as much sense as anything else in these bewildering times.

'You see?' Sister Clare whispers ecstatically. 'They're held in place by the power of the Shnax. They cannot raise a hand against those who are true.'

'This is incredible,' I croak.

'Yes,' Sister Clare says with justified satisfaction. Then she frees her hands and holds them over her head. 'We can break the circle now. Let us move among them. Show no fear. The Shnax will protect us as long as we continue to trust.'

Not all of the others look so sure about that, but they separate as ordered and edge forward.

The zombies don't budge.

'Part, sons and daughters of the darkness!' Sister Clare shrieks, swinging her right arm around like a scythe.

Not a single zombie gives ground.

One of the women loses her nerve and tries to push through, muttering sharply, 'Get out of my way!'

A zombie pulls her to the ground. He sinks his teeth into her exposed arm and tears loose a chunk of flesh. The woman screams.

'No!' Sister Clare shouts. 'Don't be afraid! Show no fear! We must be strong!'

But it's as if the scream acts as a starting pistol for the rest of the living dead. They surge forward, fingers extended, teeth bared, and throw themselves upon the stunned, defenceless children of the Shnax.

NINETEEN

The tortured death cries of the humans ring out loud. More zombies come running from within the Tube station attached to the railway concourse, not wanting to miss out on the feast.

I throw myself into the middle of the carnage and punch zombies aside, creating a narrow gap. 'This way!' I bellow.

I'm closest to Sister Clare, and she hasn't been attacked yet, so she's first past. She reels away from me and pushes through the divide, her face a mask of shock and fear. She starts to pause, but I shove her hard, careful not to pierce her flesh with my finger bones, aware that I'm as much of a threat as any revived.

'Run!' I roar at her, then try to pull some of the others free of the chaos.

Sean, the man who spoke up earlier when I was challenging Sister Clare, is the only one to get close to me. His eyes are bulging. His teeth are bared like the fangs of the monsters around us, but with terror, not hunger.

Then the finger bones of one of the zombies tear into Sean's chest, ripping through his robes, slicing into the flesh beneath. He stops and looks down at the wound. His fingers rise to touch it. All of the tension slips out of him. He smiles wearily at me, resigned to his fate. As I stare at him with horror, he spreads his arms and starts singing again. He carries on singing even when the zombies drag him down and chew through the bone of his skull, although towards the end it becomes more of a gurgling noise and the words are lost, along with the tune.

I don't stay to watch him die. As soon as I realise that the others are beyond help, I race after Sister Clare, determined to do all I can to save at least one of the nine, even though she probably deserves salvation the least of any of them.

Sister Clare was headed towards the stairs, but the zombies pouring through from the Tube station have blocked that route. As she hesitates, I call to her, 'I can see another exit at the far end. Follow me.'

We set off across the concourse. The way ahead is clear and I think we stand a chance. But then the zombies who couldn't get their hands on the other humans set their sights on Sister Clare and me — in the chaos, they won't be able to tell me apart from one of the living, so they'll tear into me too if they catch us.

A couple of seconds later it's clear we can't make it. Zombies stream into the path ahead of us, blocking the way. I draw to a halt and Sister Clare runs into my back. She tries to break past but I stop her.

'We're trapped.'

'No!' she screams. 'You've got to save me! Don't let me die!'

'I thought you were happy to die,' I grunt, but bitterness won't do either of us any good. I look around desperately as the zombies close in. There's a row of shops to our right. The doors of most are wide open and the shops are totally indefensible. But a security grille has been pulled down over the front of one shop. It doesn't hang all the way to the ground, which means it isn't locked.

'There!' I yell, darting towards the shop. Sister Clare scurries along behind me. The zombies aren't much further back.

No time to mess about. I throw myself to the floor and push up the grille. As Sister Clare ducks and skids forward, I roll, slam down the grille and leap to my feet.

'I need something to hold this in place!' I shout, but Sister Clare is moaning, lying in a huddle on the floor, hands clamped over her ears. With a curse, I look around and spot a broom with a wooden handle. Grabbing it, I stick it through one of the slots in the grille, then jam it against the wall. It wouldn't hold back any thinking person for more than a few seconds, but the living dead aren't as sharp as they once were. Ignorant of the broom, they tug on the grille, trying to force it up, unable to figure out why it isn't moving.

I back away from the grille and sink to the floor beside Sister Clare. I stare at the zombies glumly. The broom won't hold for long. They'll push through in a minute or two and that will be the end of the human. Probably the end of me as well. The zombies are in a feeding frenzy. I'm guessing they won't pause to assess me, just dig straight into my skull and tear my brain out.

Sister Clare seems to realise she's still alive and lowers her hands, looking up with startled, fearful eyes. When she sees the zombies struggling with the grille, she smiles hopefully. 'You've stopped them.'

'Only for a while. If you want to pray to your aliens, you'd better be quick.'

'There must be a lock for the grille somewhere,' she pants, looking around frantically.

I snort. 'Even if we could find it and lock ourselves in, what's the point? They won't leave as long as they can hear your heartbeat and smell your brain. Better to die quickly and get it over with, rather than sit here and starve.'

'But there might be a way out the back.'

'We're underground,' I remind her. 'My finger bones are tough, but they can't burrow through walls.'

Sister Clare makes a low moaning noise, then grabs my

arm and glares at me with some of her old determination. 'Then you have to convert me.'

'What?' I frown.

'Make me like you.' She points at the hole in my chest and the bones jutting out of my fingers. 'You're different. You can think and speak. If I end up like you, I can continue with my work.'

'*Continue?* ' I splutter.

'We were weak,' she says. 'They attacked because they sensed our fear. If I was like you, I need not fear them. I could bring others here and they'd feed on my strength and certainty. We would triumph.'

'Are you even crazier than I thought?' I shout. 'You've already led eight people to their death. How many more do you want to sacrifice?'

'As many as the Shnax demand,' she snaps. 'They wish to save us, but they can only do that if we're strong. Please, help me, don't let me be eaten, give me the power to continue with my mission.'

'Even if I wanted to, I couldn't. I don't know how –'

'Please!' she screams, not wanting to hear the truth, clasping her hands over her ears again.

I stare at the deranged woman, lost for words. Then a cruel part of me whispers, *Why not? She's doomed anyway. She lured her followers to their death and made fools of them. It's only fitting that you should do the same to her.*

'All right,' I tell her, pulling her hands away from her ears. 'We'll do it if you're sure. Are you?'

'Yes,' she gasps.

'Then on your own head be it,' I snarl, and pull her in close, as if to kiss her. But instead I bite into her lower lip, drawing blood and infecting her with my undead germs.

'Vile girl!' Sister Clare snaps, pushing me away and wiping blood from her lip. 'How dare you press your mouth to mine! I should . . .'

She raises a hand to slap me. Then she realises what I've done and backs away, whimpering softly, staring at the blood on her fingers.

'You bit me,' she whispers.

'Yeah,' I say, feeling rotten now that the moment has passed.

'Will I retain my senses?' she cries. 'Will I become like you, not like *them*?' She points at the zombies pulling at the grille.

'Of course,' I lie, not knowing if it's true or not, wanting to give her some comfort in her final moments.

'Wonderful,' she sighs, leaning against the wall, waiting for the change, probably privately plotting her undead takeover of the world.

Sister Clare shudders. She bends over, gasps, collapses, then screams as her body starts to shut down. I turn away, not wanting to see her teeth lengthen, the bones break through her fingertips, the light fade from her eyes.

The handle of the broom snaps. The grille clatters upwards. Zombies spill into the shop and swarm around us.

But they don't attack, because they can see the human turning. That makes them pause and they sniff me rather than strike. When they realise I'm one of them, they leave us be and return to the concourse, disappointed and hungry.

After about a minute, I look around guiltily. Sister Clare is staring at me numbly, no hint of life in her expression, green moss already sprouting from the bite mark on her lip.

'Sorry,' I murmur. 'But you did ask for it.'

Making a sighing sound, I blow a regretful kiss to the shadowy remains of Sister Clare, then push through the undead crowd outside the shop, patiently easing my way clear of the crush, past the bodies of the humans who were killed, up the stairs and back into the light of a world which seems even more lost and disturbing than it did an hour or two before.

TWENTY

I make my way west, then hole up in an abandoned coffee shop on Fleet Street when night falls. Every time I think about Sister Clare and her pack of nutjobs – and I think about them lots over the course of the night – I wince sadly. What a waste of life.

I feel guilty too, for biting Sister Clare, knowing it was almost certain that she wouldn't end up like me, that she'd become just another mindless revived.

'The zombies would have killed me if I hadn't done it,' I whisper.

'*So?*' I snort.

'I needed to get out,' I argue, 'to hand myself over to the soldiers, so that they can use my blood to maybe find a way to defeat the zombies.'

'*Yeah,*' I retort cynically. '*If they don't shoot me first.*'

'I've got to think positively.'

'*In this world?*' I sneer. '*Get real!*'

The night passes slowly. I hear the dead milling around outside, searching for prey, but no screams or gunfire. If any of the living are heading towards the centre to be rescued, they're lying low like me. That's not surprising. Only the cunning will have lasted this long. Smart operators like that are hardly going to give themselves away cheaply this close to escape.

As the sun rises and the zombies return to the shadows, I move out and push on, hitting the Strand. Finding a radio in a shop, I tune into the news channel and wait. It's not long before an excited presenter says that the rescue is scheduled for midday in Trafalgar Square. He tells anyone who is listening to make sure they're present at twelve on the dot, but not to show themselves in the square before that, in case they attract unwanted attention.

I head down the Strand, taking my time. I swing right and check out Covent Garden, once a throng of tourists, shoppers and street performers. I'm half-hoping to find some zombie jugglers, maybe throwing limbs around instead of skittles or juggling balls, but the place is as dead as any other part of London.

I pick up new clothes for myself in one of the fashionable designer shops, so that I look fresh and clean. I think about tearing a hole in my jumper and T-shirt, to expose the empty cavity, but decide to leave it as it is for the moment, so that I can get close to the soldiers before they realise I'm a zombie.

I file down my teeth and the bones sticking out of my fingers and toes. The bones are harder to disguise than the hole in my chest. I pull on a pair of shoes which are three sizes too big for me, and gloves that are more suited to a giant. The shoes are uncomfortable, and the gloves won't hide the shape of the bones up close, but they should get me near and give me a chance to make my case.

I also pick up a pair of watches which would have cost almost as much as our flat in the old days. They're accurate to the smallest fraction of a second, resistant to shock, waterproof, and they automatically adjust for summer or winter time. I attach one to either wrist, so that I can be absolutely sure of the time. I don't want to miss my shot at rescue because of a dodgy watch!

I get to Trafalgar Square five minutes before midday. I'm not the first to arrive. Seven people are already present, three men, a woman with a baby, a girl of eight or nine and a boy a bit younger than me. They're huddled together in the middle of the square, between the two fountains, ignoring the warning not to arrive earlier than twelve. I was expecting warriors, tough men in leathers, carrying guns. But this lot look like any group of tourists that you would have seen here a year ago.

'Are you one of us?' the woman with the baby shouts when she spots me striding towards them.

'That depends — who are you?' I shout back.

They relax at the sound of my voice. They obviously don't know about talking zombies or they wouldn't be so trusting.

Others come out of the shadows as I draw closer to the group in the centre. Two from the direction of the Mall, one from behind the Fourth Plinth, three more – not together, but separately – from Whitehall. They approach cautiously, checking out the buildings as they creep along, keeping to the middle of the road.

I was worried that the people at the heart of the square might grow suspicious if I kept my distance, but to my relief the other newcomers hang back too, not willing to associate too closely with strangers, ready to make a break for freedom if anything goes wrong.

There's no cheerful banter. Apart from the seven in the middle, who mutter among themselves, nobody speaks. Everyone looks wary, studying the others suspiciously, scanning the buildings around the square for signs of life — or, to be more accurate, *un*life.

At twelve o'clock exactly, four helicopters buzz into view overhead. They're military vehicles, armed with missiles and machine guns.

The helicopters do a few circuits over the square,

checking to make sure that everyone beneath them is human. Some of the people cheer and wave. I don't. I'm not sure if the soldiers will view me as a friend or an enemy, so I don't want to draw their scrutiny until I have to.

Satisfied with what they see, three of the helicopters set down on the terrace at the top of the steps, between the square and the National Gallery. The fourth remains airborne, hovering ominously, the pilot keeping watch over the others, ready to support them from the air if necessary.

Four soldiers slide out of each helicopter. The pilots remain in place, engines running, rotors whirring. The noise is deafening, especially with my advanced sense of hearing. I grit my teeth and try not to show any signs of distress, not wanting to appear different to the other survivors.

The twelve soldiers advance to the top of the steps. Everyone in the square has started moving towards them. A couple of people are running. But before anyone can set foot on the stairs, two of the soldiers open fire with their rifles and spray the steps with bullets.

As we come to a shocked halt, one of the soldiers moves forward and addresses us through a megaphone.

'No need to panic, people,' he barks. 'We've done this before, so we know what we're doing. We're going to get all of you out of here, but there are rules you have to obey. We've put them in place for your safety as well as ours, to ensure no infected specimens sneak through.'

'We're not infected!' one of the men yells. 'You can see that by looking at us!'

'Looks can be deceptive,' the soldier replies. 'We don't take risks. I'm sure you can appreciate our position, and the fact that the more cautiously we proceed, the safer you'll all be. We want to get you out of here as swiftly as possible, so listen up and do what you're told.'

'This is crazy!' the man roars, starting forward indignantly. 'Zombies could be closing in on us while you're wasting time. Let us through.'

'If you take one more step, sir, you *will* be executed,' the soldier snaps. As the man hesitates, he continues. 'We'll do all that we can to help you, but if we sense a threat, we'll eliminate it, no questions asked. You *do not* want to push us.'

The man gulps, raises his hands and takes three big steps back.

'OK,' the soldier says. 'Here's how it works. First you're going to undress. No need to be shy, we've seen it all before. Once you're naked, you'll approach one by one as we summon you, leaving your clothes behind. We'll check you quickly, make sure you're clean, then you can collect your gear and board the helicopters. When we've loaded everyone up, we're out of here.'

The other people grumble but begin stripping off, wanting to escape this city of the dead more than they want to protect their modesty.

I don't take off anything. Instead I wave my hands over my head and call to the soldier. 'Sir!'

The soldier smirks at me. 'I told you there was no need to be shy. Don't worry, girl, nobody's going to take photos of you.'

'That doesn't bother me. But I'm ... I'm not like the rest of them.'

His smile disappears in an instant. He takes a closer look at me, my hat, the sunglasses, the gloves and shoes.

'Take off your gloves,' the soldier growls. Something in his voice alerts the others and everybody pauses and stares at me. The soldiers adjust their guns. They're all pointing in my direction now.

'I don't want to cause any trouble,' I cry, not moving in case I set off a trigger-happy marksman.

'Remove your gloves!' the soldier with the megaphone roars.

'I will,' I moan. 'I'm doing it now.' I lower my hands and start to peel off the gloves, slow as I can. 'But you're going to see bones. And when I take off my clothes, you'll see –'

'She's infected!' a soldier shouts, and some of the people in the square start to scream.

'No!' I shriek, raising my hands again and waving them over my head. 'I want to help. I came here to offer my services.'

'Screw that,' the soldier with the megaphone snaps. 'I told you we don't take chances. Fire!'

Before I can say anything else, every soldier in the square starts shooting, and the nightmarish bellow of their guns drowns out even the ear-shattering thunder of the helicopter blades.

TWENTY-ONE

The soldiers' reaction hasn't come as a complete shock. I hoped this wouldn't happen but I half-expected it. So when I was edging forward a few minutes ago, I carefully positioned myself by one of the fountains, just in case.

As the soldiers rain down hell on me, I hurl myself to my right, into the dried-out fountain. The bullets pound the base. Stone chips and splinters fly in all directions and the piercing whine makes me gasp with pain. But I'm safe for the moment. They can't hit me from where they are, not unless I do something stupid like stick my head up.

The soldiers stop firing and the one with the megaphone shouts at the rest of the people. 'This is why we have rules! Get your damn clothes off as quick as you can or we'll shoot the lot of you!'

'We didn't know she was one of them!' a woman screams.

'We'd never seen her before. She spoke to us. How can she speak if she's dead?'

'The dead have all sorts of tricks up their sleeves,' the soldier says. 'Now show us your flesh, and hurry, before the noise brings scores of curious zombies down upon us.'

While the people are undressing, I roar at the soldiers, 'There's no need to do this. I want to help. If you don't want my help, fine, I'll leave you be. But I'm different to the other zombies. Maybe you can take some of my blood and –'

'I don't want to hear it!' the soldier yells. 'Just shut up and play dead, you damn zombie bitch!'

'Up yours, numbnuts!' I retort angrily.

'Right, that's enough,' he snarls, then barks a command into his radio.

Overhead, the airborne helicopter buzzes forward. I've seen enough war movies to know what's coming next. With a yelp, I throw myself out of the fountain. My right shoe flew from my foot when I leapt in, and now my left drops away too. But the shoes are the least of my worries. Because as I scramble clear, the pilot hits a button and launches a missile.

The fountain explodes behind me and I'm tossed clear across the square by the force of the explosion. I slam into a lamp post and slump to the ground. My ears are ringing. The hat and glasses have been blown from my head. I'm half-blind and all the way shaken.

Sitting up in a wounded daze, I catch a blurred glimpse of

the helicopter gliding in for the kill. I've nowhere to hide now and no strength to push myself towards safety even if I did. Spitting out thick, congealed blood, I sneer at the pilot – just a vague, ghostly figure from here – and give him the finger, the only missile in my own personal arsenal.

There's another explosion. I can't shut my eyes against it, so I cover them with a scratched, bloodied hand instead. Flames lick across the sky and I feel like I'm being sunburnt in the space of a few sizzling seconds. There's a roaring, maniacal sound, as if two huge sheets of welded-together metal are being wrenched apart. Then the dull thudding noises of an impossibly heavy rainfall.

None of this makes sense. The second explosion should have been the end of me. B Smith blown to bits — goodbye, cruel world. But I'm still alive and there's a gap in the sky where the helicopter should be. What the hell?

Lowering my hand, I peer through a dust cloud which has risen in front of me like a shroud. As it starts to clear, I see the wreckage of the helicopter scattered across the ground, mixed in with the remains of the fountain. Some bones jut out of the mess, all that's left of the pilot and any soldiers who were with him.

I gawp at the bewildering scene, then look up at the steps. And that's when everything clicks into sudden, sickening focus.

A second armed force has spilled out of the National

Gallery. Dozens of people, more appearing by the second, racing down the steps at the side of the pillared entrance, or leaping over the railing to land directly on the terrace. One of them has a bazooka. Smoke is spiralling from its muzzle.

The troops spewing out of the art museum are neither human nor zombies. Most are wearing jeans and hoodies. Their skin is disfigured, purple in places, peeling away from the bone in others, full of ugly, pus-filled wounds and sores. They have straggly grey hair and pale yellow eyes. I can't see from here, but I know that inside their mouths their few remaining teeth are black and stained, their tongues scabby and shrivelled, and if they spoke, the words would come out snarled and gurgled.

These are the mutants I spotted in the Imperial War Museum shortly before the zombie uprising, the same monstrous creatures who stormed the underground complex. I know no more about them now than I did then, except for two things. One — they cause chaos whenever they appear. Two — they're led by a foul being even weirder than they are.

As if on cue, as the mutants tear into the startled soldiers, I spot him emerging behind them, colourful as a peacock set against the grey backdrop of the National Gallery. He stands between two pillars, arms spread wide, grinning insanely, the pink, v-shaped gouges carved into the flesh between his eyes and lips visible even from here, through the dust and with my poor eyes.

I can't see the badge that he wears on his chest, the one with his name on it. But I know that if I could, it would read, as it did when I first met him underground on that night of spiders and death, *Mr Dowling*.

Send in the clown!

TWENTY-TWO

The mutants swarm round the soldiers and helicopters. They're soon joined by a pack of zombies, who follow them out of the National Gallery, shaded from the sun by long, *Matrix*-style leather jackets, huge straw hats and sunglasses. I'm sure the jackets, hats and glasses were chosen for them by Mr Dowling.

Two of the helicopters are overrun before their pilots can react. The third manages to clear the ground, but then the mutant with the bazooka reloads, takes aim and fires. It comes crashing back to earth, taking out the bottom section of a building where a bookshop once stood.

The soldiers fight doggedly, first with their guns, then with knives and their hands. But there are too many mutants and zombies. Within a minute the last of the human troops has been cut down and Trafalgar Square belongs to Mr Dowling and his warped warriors.

A few of the people who came to be rescued have made a break for freedom. They race from the square, hounded by a handful of whooping mutants and hungry zombies. The others are huddled together in the centre, surrounded, trapped, alive for the moment but undoubtedly doomed.

Some of the zombies focus on the humans and move in for the kill, but stop when a mutant blows a whistle. I've seen this before — Mr Dowling's henchmen have the power to command the living dead.

The mutants jeer at the weeping, shrieking humans and stab playfully at them with knives and spears, not interested in wounding them, just in winding them up. I want to try and help, cause a disturbance, break through their ranks and create a gap for the others to escape through. But I can only sit, dazed, ears ringing, legs useless, and watch.

Mr Dowling trots down the steps of the National Gallery at last, doing a little dance as he descends. The mutants applaud wildly and screech at the humans to clap too.

As the clown nimbly waltzes down the steps from the terrace to the square, I get a clearer look at him. The flesh of a severed face hangs from each shoulder of his jacket. Lengths of human guts are wrapped round his arms, and severed ears are pinned to his trouser legs. A baby's skull sticks out of the end of each of his ridiculously large red shoes. His hair is all different sorts of colours and lengths, torn from the heads of others in clumps and stapled into place. The flesh around his eyes has been cut away and filled in with soot. Two v-shaped channels run from just under either eye, down to his upper lip, and the bone beneath has been painted pink. A human eye has been stuck to the end of his nose and little red stars are dotted around it.

The trapped humans stop screaming as the clown approaches and the mutants pull back to let him through. Like me, these people have seen a lot since the world went to hell, but nothing like this. Mr Dowling belongs to another dimension entirely, one even crazier and more twisted than this undead hellhole.

To conclude his dance, Mr Dowling leaps into the air and pirouettes, then drops to one knee and spreads his arms wide. The mutants howl their appreciation and stamp their feet raucously. One of them holds up a sheet of paper with a large 10 scrawled across it in red.

Mr Dowling bows his head and accepts the acclaim with false humility. Then he hops back to both feet and prowls round the humans, grinning at them like a piranha, his eyes twitching insanely, skin wriggling as if insects are burrowing about beneath the flesh.

One of the mutants steps up next to the clown and blows his whistle sharply, waving an arm for silence. I could be wrong, but I think it's the one who tried to kidnap a baby in the Imperial War Museum on the day when I first learnt that this wasn't just a world of normal humans.

When all of the mutants are still, the one with the whistle addresses the sobbing people at the heart of the crush in a choked, gurgly voice.

'Ladies, gentlemen and children — it's show time! Welcome to the weird, wild, wonderful world of Mr Dowling and his amazing cohorts. Thrill to the sight of the living dead and their masters. Coo as we rip you from head to toe. Cheer as we make intricate designs out of your gooey innards. Worship as we take you to Hell and beyond.'

The mutants cheer again, but the humans only stare in bewilderment. Most of them are weeping openly.

'Please!' one of the men begs. 'Spare us! We're not ... we won't ... anything you ask of us ...'

'Hush,' the mutant frowns. 'Mr Dowling did not come here to entertain futile pleas. He came to party!'

'*Party!*' the mutants holler, shaking their fists and weapons over their heads.

When they're silent again, Mr Dowling points a long, bony finger at the woman with the baby and makes a shrill squeaking noise. The mutant next to him listens carefully, then crooks a finger at the woman and beckons her forward.

'No!' a man next to her shouts. 'Take me, not the baby!'

'As you wish,' the mutant shrugs. He blows his whistle and a pair of zombies lurch into action, grab the man and drag him to the ground. His screams ring loud around the square, but not for long.

'Now,' the mutant says pleasantly, crooking his finger at the woman again.

She stumbles forward, shaking her head, crying, clutching the baby to her chest. 'Please,' she whispers. 'Please. Please. Please.'

The mutant makes a soothing, tutting noise, then prises the baby from her and hands it to Mr Dowling. The clown takes the child with surprising gentleness and rocks it in his arms. The baby gurgles happily, unaware of the danger it's in. Mr Dowling makes another sharp, questioning noise.

'Is it a boy or a girl?' the mutant asks politely.

'A guh-guh-guh-girl,' the woman gasps, eyes on her child, fingers clasped in silent prayer, rooted to the spot, helpless and terrified.

The clown nods slowly and squeals again.

'Mr Dowling says that he's glad,' the mutant translates. 'He's not in a boyish mood today. If it had been a boy, he would have dashed its head open and fed its brain to our zombies. But since it's a girl, he's inclined to be merciful.'

'He ... he's not going to hurt her?' the woman croaks, tearing her eyes away from the baby and looking to the mutant with the slightest glimmer of hope.

'That depends on the choice you make,' the mutant says.

'*Choose* ...' the other mutants murmur. The word sounds obscene on their scabby, twisted tongues.

'I don't understand,' the woman frowns.

'It's very simple,' the mutant grins. 'The ever-generous Mr Dowling is giving you a choice. You can choose to spare your baby or your colleagues.' He nods at the other humans in the square.

'You mean . . .' She gulps, eyes widening.

'You got it, sweet thing,' the mutant chuckles obscenely. 'We butcher the baby or we kill everybody else. Your call. Now — choose.'

'*Choose . . .*' the others repeat again, their pale yellow eyes alive with repulsive yearning.

As the woman struggles with her choice, someone squats next to me and says, 'As distasteful as this is, it should be intriguing. Mr Dowling always puts on a memorable show.'

I look around in a daze. The man is tall and thin, but with a pot belly. He's wearing a striped suit with a pink shirt. He has white hair and pale skin, long fingers and unbelievably large eyes, twice the size of any normal person's, almost fully white, but with a tiny dark pupil burning fiercely at the centre of each.

'*Owl Man*,' I moan.

TWENTY-THREE

'You remember me,' the man with the owl-like eyes beams. 'How sweet.' He winks, then blows me a mocking kiss.

'This can't be real,' I mutter. 'I must be dreaming.'

'Don't be silly,' Owl Man tuts. 'You cannot sleep, so it follows that you cannot dream. Therefore this must be real.'

'It could be a hallucination.'

'Possibly,' he concedes. 'But it isn't. Now tell me, are you hurt? Can I help you?'

He reaches out a hand. I push myself away from his creepy-looking fingers and wipe dirt and blood from my forehead. 'How are you here?' I ask. 'The last time I saw you was in my bedroom.'

'There's no telling who you might run into these days,' he smiles. 'The world was always a small place, but now it's positively box-like. So few of us left with our senses intact. Our paths cannot fail to cross.'

Owl Man stands and stretches. I frown as I study him.

'What are you? I can hear your heartbeat, so you're not a zombie. But you're not a mutant either, are you?'

'Certainly not,' he says, sniffing as if offended. 'I am ...' He pauses, thinks for a moment, then shrugs. 'I am, as you so poetically put it, *Owl Man*. That is all you need to know about me for now.'

My mind is whirring. There are so many questions I want to put to him, about the mutants, Mr Dowling, why certain zombies revitalise. I've a feeling that if anyone can answer those questions, it's him.

But before I can ask Owl Man anything, the mutant with the whistle shouts at the woman faced with the impossible choice. 'Time's up. Choose or we slaughter them all, baby, adults, the lot.'

Owl Man grimaces. 'Kinslow is a nasty piece of work, but he keeps things interesting, and that's what Mr Dowling demands of his followers.'

I get the sense that Owl Man doesn't approve of what's going on. But he doesn't try to stop it, just observes the sick show with a neutral expression.

'Hurry!' the mutant called Kinslow croaks. 'Choose now or ...' He produces a knife and passes it to Mr Dowling. The clown laughs as he takes it, then slides the blade up beneath the baby's chin.

'*Them!*' the woman howls, falling to the ground with horror. 'Take them! Spare my child!'

The other people scream with fear and outrage, but their cries are cut short when Kinslow blows his whistle again, three long toots. At his command the living dead surge forward and tuck into the hapless humans, survivors no longer, just zombie fodder now.

'This is awful,' I groan, turning my gaze away.

'Yes,' Owl Man says morosely. 'But it's about to get even worse. Look.'

Mr Dowling hasn't handed back the baby. As the zombies finish off the last of the humans and tuck into fresh, warm brains, the clown strides among them, still clasping the infant. Kinslow and the woman trail after him, the mutant snickering, the woman distraught.

'My girl,' she whimpers, reaching for the baby.

'In a minute,' Kinslow snaps, pulling her back. 'You don't want to disturb Mr Dowling when he's preoccupied. You wouldn't like him if he lost his temper.'

The clown comes to a halt over a thin, male zombie who is digging into the open head of the boy who wasn't much younger than me. He watches the zombie for a while, then sticks his left index finger into a hole in the man's throat, where he was bitten when still alive. His finger comes out wet and red. With a soft, choking noise, he puts the finger into the baby's mouth and the little girl's lips close on it trustingly.

'*No!*' the girl's mother screams, sensing the threat too late to prevent it. She tries to throw herself at the clown, but Kinslow kicks her legs out from beneath her and she collapses.

'No! No! No!' she screeches, covering her ears with her hands as the baby's brittle bones extend and snap through the skin of her fingers and toes. 'You told me you'd spare her! You promised!'

'We did spare her,' Kinslow says, taking the zombie baby from Mr Dowling and holding her out to the woman who was once her mother. 'She still lives, in a fashion. She's as wriggly and alert as ever. Just a little less ... *breathy*. Now take her. She's yours to do with as you wish.'

Kinslow presses the baby into her mother's arms. Her tiny sharp teeth, newly sprouted, snap together as she stares at the woman whose brain smells so good and tempting, even to one as young as this.

The woman gazes down on her ruined child for a full minute in horrified silence, the clown and Kinslow waiting to see what she'll do next, everybody watching with wretched fascination except for the feasting zombies. Then, like a person sleepwalking, she undoes the buttons on her shirt and frees a breast. She presses her daughter to it and lets the undead baby bite and feed, murmuring softly to her, stroking her hair, vowing to care for her even in death.

'A touching scene,' Owl Man murmurs.

'Bastard,' I snarl at him.

'There's no point blaming me,' he says. 'I wasn't responsible.'

'You didn't do anything to stop it though, did you?' I challenge him.

'That's not my role,' he says. 'We all have a role to play in life, and unlike many unfortunate souls, I am all too aware of what the universe demands of me. I simply follow the path that destiny demands, as we all must.'

'Even if it means letting babies be sacrificed?' I sneer.

'Yes,' Owl Man whispers and a sad look crosses his oversized eyes. 'You may find this hard to believe, but I have done even worse than that in my time. I fear that you might too, over the course of the grim days and nights to come.'

'What are you talking about?' I snap.

'Remember when you could dream? Remember the babies on the plane?'

I shiver at the memory. Owl Man also asked me about my dreams the last time we met. 'What about the bloody nightmares?' I growl.

'They marked you, Becky,' he says. 'I was sure you would survive and regain your senses, just as I was certain we would meet again. You are a creature of the darkness, the same as myself and Mr Dowling. Like us, I fear that you too will end up destined to play a cruel, vicious part in the shaping of the future. Some of us cannot escape the damnable reach of fate.'

Before I can ask Owl Man what that means, he stands and calls to Kinslow and Mr Dowling. 'I have someone here I think you might be interested in.'

The clown bounds across, Kinslow racing to keep up. Mr Dowling stops in front of me and beams as if to welcome an old friend.

'You made it out,' Kinslow grunts, pulling up beside his master. 'Mr Dowling said that you would. You caught his eye underground. He told me you were the cream of the crop.'

'See, Becky?' Owl Man mutters. '*Marked.*'

Kinslow glares at the tall man with the owlish eyes, but says nothing.

Mr Dowling bends over until his face is in front of mine. The last time he did that, he spat a shower of spiders over me. But today I can't see anything in his mouth, only a long, black tongue.

The clown smells worse than an open sewer. My nose wrinkles and I try to turn my face away, but he grabs my chin and forces me to maintain eye contact. As he stares into my soul with his beady, twitching eyes, he squeals a few times, softly.

'He wants to know if you're ready to come with us,' Kinslow says. 'He knows that you disapprove of many of the things we do. But he's willing to teach you, spend time with you, show you the way forward, share his power with you.'

'He's out of his tiny mind if he thinks I'll ever have anything to do with you lot,' I jeer. 'You're freaks, every last damn one of you. I wouldn't spit on you if you were on fire, even if I *could* spit.'

The clown tilts his head sideways and frowns.

'You should kill her for saying a thing like that,' Kinslow growls.

'Mr Dowling decides who to kill and who to spare,' Owl Man thunders, his smooth voice dropping several octaves in the space of a heartbeat, his eyes flaring. 'Don't ever forget that or speak out of turn again. He makes the calls, not you.'

'Of course,' Kinslow says quickly, fear mixed in with his apology. 'I meant no disrespect. I was merely –'

'Shut up if you want to live,' Owl Man says lazily, then looks to the clown. 'I told you she would not come with us. Do you want to crack her skull open or let her go?'

The clown stares at me for a few seconds. Then he makes a chuckling, wheezy sound, turns and sets off across the square, Kinslow hurrying to keep up with him.

Owl Man winks at me, all smiles again. 'He said we'll probably end up killing you, but not today. He's in a good mood after the game with the baby. Go with his blessing, but bear this in mind — no matter where you go, no matter what you do, he knows you're out there and he can find you any time he likes. You haven't seen the last of Mr Dowling, Becky, not by a long shot.'

Owl Man peels away and follows the mutants and their

141

master. I watch numbly as the clown gathers his posse and leads them from the square. Someone starts to sing an old ballad about murder and revenge, and by the time they pass from sight, they've all joined in, one big, happy party, heading off in search of fresh pickings, leaving me to fester in the square, surrounded by the wreckage of the helicopters and the cooling bodies of the dead.

TWENTY-FOUR

I remain in Trafalgar Square overnight, barely moving, staring at nothing, wishing somebody would come along and free me from this unholy hell of an existence. Zombies trail through the square over the course of the night, scraping dry the skulls of the corpses, ridding them of every last scrap of brain. Some come sniffing to make sure I'm not edible too. I ignore them and focus on the empty feeling inside, remembering the baby, the mutants, Owl Man, the clown, the bloodshed.

In the morning, as the sun rises and the carnage is revealed in all its gory glory once again, I push myself to my feet, pick up my trusty Australian hat which is lying nearby, dusty but undented, and turn my back on the grisly scene. I'm in a universe of pain, and limp badly as I shuffle away, but my wounds aren't fatal. I'll survive, worse luck.

In a numb daze, I start down Whitehall. It's not an

especially long road, but it takes me ages to get to the end, hobbling and limping, dripping occasional drops of thick, gooey blood from wounds I don't even begin to explore.

I pass Downing Street, once home to the Prime Minister. I know he didn't make it out of London alive — the news programmes mentioned his loss a few times. He hasn't been missed. His cabinet neither. The army runs the country these days.

I wonder if the PM is still inside Number Ten, a zombie like so many of his voters, resting until dark. I could check – the gate is open and unguarded – and probably would any other time. But I'm too weary to care about such trivialities. This country has fallen. Babies are being turned into zombies and feeding on their mothers. Who cares about stuffy politicians now?

Big Ben comes into view. I pause and stare glumly at the clock tower. The hands have stopped at just before a quarter to five. It doesn't chime any more. I doubt it ever will again. A dead clock at the heart of a dead city.

As I edge past the Houses of Parliament, I spot a large red z sprayed near the base of Big Ben, an arrow underneath pointing towards Westminster Bridge. I had planned to turn left and crawl along the riverbank, heading back east to more familiar territory, to see out my time on home turf. But the arrow intrigues me. I've seen others like it during my march west. I think they might be the work of Mr Dowling – he sketched a blood-red z on my cheek when he visited me in my cell in the underground bunker – but I'm not sure. Maybe they were sprayed by humans, survivors hoping to guide others to their hideout. If so, they might be more interested in my offer of assistance than the soldiers were.

Silly old B! Still keen to help the living. Will I never learn?

I move forward, wincing, dragging my left leg, half-blind and itching like crazy. I should have found new clothes and glasses before I came out on to an exposed bridge, but I wasn't thinking clearly. No matter. I push on regardless. I won't be in the sun for long. There will be plenty of shadowy corners for me to rest in on the south side of the river.

I'm surprised, as I advance, to note that the London Eye is still revolving. At first I think it's a trick of the light, so I stop and watch it for a minute. But no, the capsules are moving slowly, just as they did in the old days when every tourist in London made a beeline for its most popular attraction. Today, though, the capsules are deserted. The Eye might be open for business, but it doesn't have any takers.

As I drag myself off Westminster Bridge, I think about the London Dungeon, a place I visited several times when I was alive. I passed its original home earlier in my journey, and now here I am at its subsequent location in County Hall. Maybe that's the place for me. I'd fit in perfectly among all the waxwork monsters.

'No,' I whisper. 'You're too grisly. You'd give the rest of the freaks a bad name.'

Shuffling on, I come to the turning for Belvedere Road, which separates the buildings of County Hall, and spot another red z with an arrow beneath, pointing up the road.

I stare wearily at the arrow. I need to feed. It's been a long time since I last ate. I can feel my stomach tightening, my senses beginning to loosen. If I don't tuck into some brains soon, I'll regress and become a mindless revived. If I'm going to follow these damn arrows, I need to make sure I'm in good shape to deal with living humans if I run into any.

St Thomas's Hospital is just behind me, so I turn slowly and make for it. I assumed a hospital would offer rich pickings, but as I work my way through the wards, I find that isn't the case. Others have been here before me and scraped the remains of the corpses dry.

But I've got a bit more up top than your average zombie. As far as I know, any hospital this size has a morgue. And I'm guessing they were normally situated on one of the lower floors, so the staff didn't have to wheel corpses through the rest of the hospital, spooking the life out of everybody.

I find the morgue after a short search but it's locked. It takes me far longer to track down keys for the door, but eventually I find a set in a nurses' cabinet and let myself in. It's brighter and cleaner than I anticipated, no stench of death at all.

The morgue is refrigerated and the electricity is still working. I don't find as many corpses as I thought I might, but four are lying on slabs, ready and waiting, and there are probably a few more tucked away out of sight. If I don't stray from this area in the near future, I can come back and search again. But right now I have more than I need. Time to dine.

I mutter a quick apology over the body of a woman in her early twenties, then chip through her skull with my finger bones and prise out bits of her brain. I eat mechanically, forcing down the food. When I've eaten my fill, I let myself out, lock the door behind me, and throw up in the corridor. I place the keys back where I found them, then return to Belvedere Road, moving more easily than before, but still very far from normal. If my bones and flesh don't heal – and I've no reason to think they will – I'm going to be hobbling like this until the end. No more long jumping or sprinting for me.

I limp along, head low, feeling sorry for myself. As I come to one of the entrances into the main building of County Hall, I notice a small red z sprayed on a wall, the arrow beneath it pointing inwards. I stare at the arrow for a long time, then shrug, mount the steps and push open the unlocked door at the top. If this is a trap, so be it. I'm too tired to worry.

The shade of the building is a welcome relief after being out in the sun. To my surprise there are no zombies here. I thought a massive, dark area like this would be bursting with the undead, but I seem to be the only soul making use of the place.

I wind my way through a warren of corridors and rooms with unbelievably high ceilings. This is like a palace. I never knew there was so much to it. I've been to the aquarium and games arcade at the front of the building in the past, and the London Dungeon, of course, but had no idea that all this existed further back.

Many of the doors are shut and won't open. If I wanted to, I might be able to force them apart or find keys if I searched, but I'm content to simply wander where I can, stepping through every door that opens to me, ignoring the rest.

After a while, I come to a room overlooking the river. I edge up next to the panels of cracked glass and gaze out at one of the best views in town. To my left lie Big Ben, the Houses of Parliament and Westminster Bridge. To my right is a bridge for trains, and just beyond that, Waterloo Bridge. Huge, ornate buildings line the bank on the far side of the river. The London Eye is directly ahead of me, imposing and graceful, still turning smoothly, silently, like some wind-up toy standing tall and proud among the ruins of the city.

I take off my hat and let it drop to the floor. Rubbing the back of my neck, I lean my head against the glass and make a sighing sound. I feel more alone than ever in this immense building, like I'm in a tomb.

Then, as I'm glumly considering where I should turn next, from just behind me, out of the shadows of what was an empty room when I entered, somebody coughs politely and says, 'Good morning, Miss Smith. We've been expecting you.'

To be continued ...

THE
ZOM-B
CHRONICLES II

ZOM-B ANGELS

THEN . . .

Becky Smith was at school the day the dead came back to life and took over the world. She tried to escape with a group of friends, but it wasn't meant to be. Her heart was torn from her chest and she became a zombie.

Several months later B recovered her senses in an underground military complex. The soldiers lumped her in with the zom heads, a pack of revitalised teenagers like her who had somehow regained their minds. They were told by their captors that they had to eat brains to stay conscious, and had a life expectancy of just a couple of years.

B would probably have remained a prisoner for the rest of her days, if not for the intervention of a monstrous clown called Mr Dowling. He invaded with a team of mutants, set the zombies free and killed many of the staff. B didn't think he did it because he was pro-zombie — it looked to her like he did it for kicks.

Most of the zom heads were executed while trying to

escape, but B made it out. She thought Rage might have got away as well. He was a self-serving bully who turned on his guards and proved just as clinical and merciless as they had been, casually killing one of the scientists before setting off on his own and warning his fellow zom heads not to follow him.

B roamed the streets of London for a while, mourning the loss of the normal world. It was a city of the dead, dotted with just a handful of living survivors. Some had chosen to stay, but others were trapped and desperately searching for a way out.

When B heard that the army was mounting a rescue operation, she went to offer herself to them, figuring they might be able to use her DNA to help other zombies recover their minds. But the soldiers saw her as a threat and tried to kill her. Once again the killer clown saved her. He slaughtered the humans, then asked her if she wanted to join him. B could think of nothing worse than teaming up with Mr Dowling, his creepy mutants and an eerie guy with owl-like eyes who had shown an interest in her even before the zombies attacked. She told him to stick his offer.

Wounded, bewildered and alone, B wandered across the river and staggered into an old building, County Hall, once the home of local government, now a deserted shell. At least that was what it looked like. But as B stared out of a window at the river, a man called to her by name and said he had been waiting for her.

NOW . . .

ONE

I whirl away from the window that overlooks the Thames. A man has entered the room through a door which I didn't notice on my way in. He's standing in the middle of the open doorway, arms crossed, smiling.

My survival instinct kicks in. With a roar, I hurl myself at the stranger, ignoring the flare of pain in my bruised, broken body. I curl my fingers into a fist and raise my hand over my head as I close on him.

The man doesn't react. He doesn't even uncross his arms. All he does is cock his head, to gaze with interest at my raised fist. His smile never slips.

I come to a stop less than a metre from the man, eyeing him beadily as my fist quivers above my head. If he'd tried to defend himself, I would have torn into him, figuring he was an enemy, as almost everybody else in this city seems to be. But he leaves himself open to attack and continues to smile.

'Who the hell are you?' I snap. He's dressed in a light grey suit, a white shirt and purple tie, and expensive-looking leather shoes. He has thin hair, neatly combed back, brown but streaked with grey. Calm brown eyes. Looks like he's in his forties.

'I am Dr Oystein,' he introduces himself.

'That supposed to mean something to me?' I grunt.

'I would be astonished if it did,' he says, then extends his right hand.

'You don't want to shake hands with me,' I sneer. 'Not unless you want to end up with a taste for brains.'

'I was an adventurous diner in my youth,' Dr Oystein says, his smile widening. 'I often boasted that I would eat the flesh or innards of just about any creature, except for humans. Alas, ironically, I can now eat nothing else.'

I frown and focus on his fingers. Bones don't stick out of them the way they poke out of every other zombie's, but now that I look closely, I see that the flesh at the tips is broken, a small white mound of filed-down bone at the centre of each pink whorl.

'Yes,' he says in answer to my unvoiced question. 'I am undead like you.'

I still don't take his hand. Instead I focus on his mouth. His teeth are nowhere near as jagged or as long as mine, but they're not the same as a normal person's either.

Dr Oystein laughs. 'You are wondering how I keep my

teeth in such good shape, but there is no magic involved. I have been in this lifeless state a lot longer than you. One develops a knack for these things over time. I was brought up to believe that a gentleman should be neatly groomed and I have found myself as fastidious in death as I once was in life.

'Please take my hand, Becky. I will feel very foolish if you do not.'

'I don't give a monkey's how you feel,' I snort, and instead of shaking his hand, I listen closely for his heartbeat. When I don't detect one, I relax slightly.

'How do you know my name?' I growl. 'How could you have been expecting me? I didn't know that I was coming to County Hall. I wandered in randomly.'

Dr Oystein shakes his head. 'I have come to believe that nothing in life is truly random. In this instance it definitely was no coincidence that you wound up here. You were guided by the signs, as others were before you.'

I think back and recall a series of spray-painted, z-shaped symbols with arrows underneath. I've been following the arrows since I left the East End, sometimes because they happened to be pointing the way that I was travelling, but other times deliberately.

'Z for zombie,' Dr Oystein says as he sees my brain click. 'The signs mean nothing to reviveds, but what curious revitalised could turn a blind eye to such an intriguing mystery?'

165

'You know about reviveds and revitaliseds?'

'Of course.' He coughs lightly. 'In fact I was the one who coined the terms.'

'Who are you?' I whisper. '*What* are you?'

Dr Oystein sighs. 'I am a scientist and teacher. A sinner and gentleman. A killer and would-be saviour. And, if you will do me the great honour, I would like to be your friend.'

The mysterious doctor waves his extended arm, once again inviting me to accept his hand. And this time, after a brief hesitation, even though I'm still suspicious, I lower my fist, uncurl my fingers and shake hands with the politely-spoken zombie.

TWO

'You have a strange accent,' I remark as Dr Oystein releases my hand. 'Where are you from?'

'Many places,' he says, slowly circling me, examining my wounds. 'My father was English but my mother was Norwegian. I was born in Norway and lived there for a while. Then my parents moved around Europe – my father had itchy feet – and I, of course, travelled with them.'

I try not to jitter as the doctor slips behind me. If he's been concealing a weapon, he'll be able to whip it out and strike. My shoulders tense as I imagine him driving a long knife between them. But he doesn't attack, just continues to circle, and soon he's facing me again.

'I heard that your heart had been ripped out,' he says. 'May I see?'

'How do you know that?' I scowl.

'I had contacts in the complex where you were previously

incarcerated. I know much about you, but I hope to learn more. Please?' He nods towards my top.

With a sigh, I grab the hem of my T-shirt and lift it high, exposing my chest. Dr Oystein stares at the cavity on the left, where my heart once beat. Now there's just a jagged hole, rimmed by congealed blood and a light green moss.

'Fascinating,' the doctor murmurs. 'We zombies are all freaks of nature, each a walking medical marvel, but one tends to forget that. This is a reminder of our ability to defy established laws. You are a remarkable individual, Becky Smith, and you should be proud of the great wound which you bear.'

'Stop it,' I grunt. 'You'll make me blush.'

Dr Oystein sniffs. 'Not unless you are even more remarkable than the rest of us. Without a heart, how would your body pump blood to your pale, pretty cheeks?'

Dr Oystein makes a gesture, inviting me to lower my T-shirt. As I do so, he steps across to the window where I was standing when he first addressed me. County Hall boasts one of the best views in the city. He looks out at the river, the London Eye, the Houses of Parliament and all the other deserted buildings.

'Such devastation,' he mumbles. 'You must have encountered horrors beyond your worst nightmares on your way to us. Am I correct?'

I think about all of the corpses and zombies I've seen . . .

Mr Dowling and the people he tormented and killed in Trafalgar Square ... his army of mutants and his bizarre sidekick, Owl Man ... the hunters who almost killed me ... Sister Clare of the Order of the Shnax, the way she transformed when I bit her ...

'You're not bloody wrong,' I wheeze.

'The world teeters on the brink,' Dr Oystein continues. 'It has been dealt a savage blow and I am sure that most of those who survived believe that there is no way back, regardless of what the puppets of the military might say in their radio broadcasts.'

'You've heard those too?'

'Oh yes. I tune in whenever I am in need of bittersweet amusement.' He looks back at me. 'There are many fools in this world, and it is no crime to be one of them. But to try and carry on as normal when all around you has descended into chaos ... to try to convince others that you can restore order by operating as you did before ... That goes beyond mere foolishness. That is madness and it will prove the true downfall of this world if we leave these people to their sad, petty, all too human devices.

'There *is* hope for civilisation as we once knew it. But if the living are to rise again, they will need our help, since only the conscious undead stand any sort of chance against the brain-hungry legions of the damned.'

Dr Oystein beckons me forward. I shuffle towards him

slowly, not just because of the pain, but because I've almost been mesmerised by his words. He speaks like a hypnotist, slow, assured, serious.

When I join him at the window, Dr Oystein points to the London Eye, turning as smoothly and steadily as it did when thousands of tourists flocked there every day.

'I consider that a symbol of all that has been lost but which might one day be restored,' the doctor says. 'We keep it going, day and night, a beacon of living hope in this city of the dead. But no ordinary human could operate the Eye — they would be sniffed out and besieged by zombies. We, on the other hand, can. The dead will not bother us, since we are of no interest to them. That lack of interest is our strength and humanity's only hope of once again taking control of this planet.

'You are not the first revitalised to find your way here,' Dr Oystein goes on. 'There are others – weary, battered warriors – who have crawled through the streets of bloodshed and nightmares in search of sanctuary and hope, following the signs as you did.'

'Are you talking about zom heads?' I ask.

'Yes,' he says. 'But we do not use that term here. If you choose to stay with us and work for the forces of justice and mercy, you will come to think of yourself as we do, not as a zom head but an *Angel*.'

I snort. 'With wings and a harp? Pull the other one!'

'No wings,' Dr Oystein smiles. 'No harp either. But an Angel nonetheless.' He moves away from the window, towards the door. 'I have much to show you, Becky. You do not have to accompany me – you are free to leave any time that you wish, and always will be – but, if you are willing, I will take you on a tour and reveal some of the many secrets of the newly redefined County Hall.'

I stare at the open doorway. It's shadowy in the corridor outside. There could be soldiers waiting to jump me and stick me in a cell again.

'Why should I trust you?' I ask.

Dr Oystein shrugs. 'I could tell you to listen to your heart, but ...'

The grisly joke eases my fears. Besides, there's no way I could turn back now. He's got me curious and, like a cat, I have to follow my nose and hope it doesn't lead me astray.

'All right, doc,' I grunt, limping over to him and grinning, as if I haven't a care in the world. 'You can be my guide. Just don't expect a tip at the end.'

'I will ask for no tip,' he says softly. 'But I *will* ask for your soul.' He smiles warmly as I stiffen. 'There's no need to be afraid. When the time comes, I believe you will give it to me gladly.'

And with that cryptic remark, he leads me out of the room of light and into the vast, dark warren beyond.

THREE

'This is an amazing building,' Dr Oystein says as we wander through a series of long corridors, popping into massive, ornately decorated rooms along the way. 'Four thousand people worked here at its zenith. To think that it is now home to no more than a few dozen ...' He makes a sighing sound.

'I came here a few times when I was younger,' I tell him. 'I went on the Eye, visited the aquarium and the London Dungeon, hung out in the arcade, ate at some of the restaurants. My dad brought us up one New Year's Eve for the fireworks. We queued for ages to get a drink from a shop nearby. Worth it though — it was a cool show.'

Dr Oystein pushes open a door to reveal a room with a handful of beds. They haven't been made up and I get the sense that nobody is using them.

'I had no idea how many revitaliseds would find their way

to us,' he says. 'I hoped for many, feared for few, but we prepared for an influx to be on the safe side. There are many rooms like this, waiting for teenagers like you who will in all likelihood never come.'

I frown. 'Why just teenagers? Don't you accept adults too?'

'We would if any came, but adult revitaliseds are rare.'

'Why?' I ask.

'I will explain later,' he promises.

He closes the door and pushes on. After a while the style of the corridors and rooms changes and I realise we've crossed into one of the hotels which were part of County Hall before the zombie uprising.

'Oh, for the simple comforts of life,' Dr Oystein says drily as we check out a suite that's bigger than my family's old flat in the East End. 'Did you ever stay in a hotel like this, Becky?'

'No. And it's B,' I tell him. 'That's what everybody calls me.'

'Is that what you prefer?'

'Yeah.'

He nods. 'As you wish. We all have the right to choose our own name.'

'How about you?' I counter. 'Dr Oystein's a mouthful. What's your first name?'

He smiles. 'Oystein *is* my first name. It has been so long

since I used my surname that I have almost forgotten what it is.'

We double back on ourselves, but take a different route. This place is a maze. My head is spinning as I try to chart all the twists and turns, in case I need to make a quick getaway. The doctor seems like a nice old bloke, but I'm taking nothing for granted.

'How many rooms are there?' I ask.

'Far too many to count,' Dr Oystein says. 'We use very few of them. It's a pity we cannot make more use of the space, but we do not have the numbers at the moment. Maybe one day we can bring it fully back to life, but for the time being we must rattle around in it.'

'Why don't you move somewhere smaller?'

Dr Oystein coughs as if embarrassed. 'To be honest, I always had a fondness for County Hall. When I was casting around for a base, this was my first choice. The Angels seem to share my love for the building. I hope that it will come to feel like home for you over time, as it has for us.'

'So who lives here with you?' I ask. 'You haven't told me about the set-up yet, how you came to be here, who your Angels are, how you plan to save the world.'

'Those questions will all be answered,' he assures me. 'We do not keep secrets from one another. We are open in all that we do. But there is no need to rush. As you adjust and settle in, we will reveal more of our work and background to you, until you know as much about us as I do.'

I don't like being told to wait, but this is his gig. Besides, I'm exhausted and my brain hurts, so I don't think I could take in much more anyway. There's one thing that does disturb me though, and I want to bring it up before pushing on any further.

'How come there are no regular zombies here? Every other big, dark building that I've seen has been packed with them.'

'I had already recruited a small team of Angels before I established a permanent base,' he says. 'We drove out the reviveds before we moved in.'

'That must have been messy.'

'It was actually the easiest thing in the world,' he replies. 'With their sharp sense of hearing, reviveds – like revitaliseds – are vulnerable to high-pitched noises. So we simply installed a few speakers and played a string of high notes through them, which proved unbearable for those who had taken up residence. They moved out without any protest, then we slid in after them and shored up the entrances.'

'I got in without any hassle,' I remind him.

'We saw you coming on our security cameras,' he says. 'We switched off the speakers – we repositioned them around the building once we had moved in, and normally play the noises on a constant loop, to keep stray reviveds at bay – and made sure a door was open when you arrived.'

We come to a huge room and I catch my first glimpse of what I assume are some of Dr Oystein's Angels. There's a small group of them at the centre of the room, in a boxing ring, sparring. They're my sort of age, no more than a year or two older or younger than me.

'They spend most of their days training,' Dr Oystein says.

'For what?'

'War.'

I swivel to look at him, but he doesn't return my gaze.

'The years ahead will be hard,' he says quietly. 'We will be tested severely, and I am sure at times we will be found wanting. We face many battles, some of which we are certain to lose. But if we prepare as best we can, and have faith in ourselves and the justness of our cause, we will triumph in the end.'

I snort. 'I hate to burst your bubble, doc, but if those Angels are like me, you'd better tell them to get their arses in gear. In another year or two we'll be pushing up daisies. You can't win a war if all your troops are rotting in the grave.'

Dr Oystein frowns. 'What are you talking about?'

'Our limited lifespan. We've only got a year and a half, two years max. Then our senses will dissolve, our brains will melt and we'll be dead meat. If you've got a war you want to win, you'd better crack on and –'

'You were told many things when you were a prisoner,'

Dr Oystein interrupts. 'Some were true. Some, you must surely know, were not. Your captors wanted to bend you to their will. They told you lies to dampen your spirit, to break it, to make you theirs.'

I stare at him, hardly daring to believe what he's telling me. 'You mean it was bullshit about me only having a year or two to live?'

'Of the highest grade,' he smiles.

'I'm not going to die soon?' I cry.

'You are already dead,' he says.

'You know what I mean,' I groan. 'My brain's not going to pop and leave me truly dead?'

'Far from it.'

I clench my fingers tight and give the air a victory punch. 'Bloody *YES*, mate! You've made my day, doc. I was ready to accept an early end, but as crap as my excuse for a life is, I'd rather this than no life at all.'

'Most of us share your view,' he chuckles, then grows serious. 'But they did not tell you a total lie. We do not age the same way that humans do. Our lifespan, for want of a better term, is not what an average human might expect.'

'So it was half true,' I growl. 'Those are the best sort of lies, I guess. Go on then, doc, hit me with the bad news. I can take it. How long do I have? Twenty years? Ten? Five?'

'We cannot be absolutely certain,' he says. 'I have run many tests and made a series of predictions. But we have no long-term data to analyse, and will not have for many decades to come. There are all sorts of genetic kinks of which I might be ignorant.'

'Your guess is better than mine,' I smile. 'I won't blame you if you're off by a few years.'

'Very well. I won't tease you with a dramatic build-up. As I said, this is a rough estimate, but based on the results of my tests to date, I think we probably have a life expectancy of between two and three thousand years.

'And no,' he adds before I can say anything, 'I'm not joking.' He leans in close, his eyes wide as I stare at him, stunned and numb. 'So, B Smith, what do you think of this *crap life* now?'

FOUR

I'm in shock for ages. To go from thinking you have only months to live, to being told you might be hanging around for a couple of millennia ... it's a cataclysmic leap and my mind whirls as we continue the tour.

We visit a kitchen where a good-looking, stylishly dressed woman with a big smile is scraping brains from inside severed human heads and dumping them in a mixing bowl. Dr Oystein introduces us, but I forget the woman's name even before we leave the room.

'Some of the heads are delivered to us from people who die of natural causes in human compounds,' he says. 'We have contacts among the living who view us as allies, and they give us what they can. But most come from fresh corpses that we found in morgues or dug up not long after the first zombie attacks. I knew brains would be a pressing issue, so I made them my number-one priority. For a couple

of weeks, grave-robbing was practically our full-time occu-
pation.'

He tells me how he's trying to create a synthetic substitute
that will give us the nutrients we need, so that we don't have
to rely on reaping brains from dead humans in future, but
I'm barely listening.

More bedrooms, another training centre – again, I only
spot teenagers – and the impressive council chamber. Dr
Oystein starts waffling on about the history of County Hall,
but I can't focus. I keep thinking about the centuries stretch-
ing out ahead of me, the incredibly long life that has been
dropped on me without any warning.

Halfway down another of the building's long corridors, I
stop and shake my head. 'This is crazy,' I shout. 'You're
telling me I'm gonna live at least twenty times longer than
any human?'

'Yes,' Dr Oystein says calmly.

'How the hell can anyone last that long?'

He shrugs. 'A living person could not. But we are dead.
We do not age as we used to. If we take care of our bodies,
and sustain ourselves by eating brains, we can defy the laws
of living flesh.'

'Then what's to say we won't live forever?' I challenge
him. 'Where did you pull two or three thousand years from?
If we don't age –'

'We *do* age,' he cuts in smoothly. 'I said that we do not age as we used to, but we definitely age, only at a much slower rate. Our external appearance will not change much, except for scarring, wrinkling and discolouring. Our internal organs are to all intents and purposes irrelevant, so even if they crumble away, it won't really matter.

'Only our brains are susceptible to the ravages of time. From what my tests have revealed, they are slowly deteriorating. If they continue to fail at the rate I have noted in the subjects that I have been able to assess, we should manage to hold ourselves together for two or three thousand years. But it could be less, it could be more. Only time will tell.'

I shake my head again, still struggling to come to terms with the revelation.

'Try not to think about it too much,' Dr Oystein says kindly. 'I know it is a terrifying prospect — a long life seems enviable until one is presented with the reality of it and has to think of all those days and nights to come, how hard it will be to fill them, to keep oneself amused for thousands of years. And it is even harder since we do not sleep and thus have more time to deal with than the living.

'But as with everything in life, you will learn to cope. I'm not saying it will be easy or that you won't have moments of doubt, but I suggest you turn a blind eye to your longevity for now. You can brood about it later.' He sighs. 'There will be plenty of time for brooding.'

'Why tell me about it at all if that's the case?' I snap.

Dr Oystein shrugs. 'It is important that you know. It is one of the first things that I tell my Angels. Our approach to life – or our semblance of it – differs greatly depending on how much time we have to play with.'

'Come again?' I frown.

'If you think you have only a year to live, you might behave recklessly, risking life and limb, figuring you have little to lose. Most people treat their bodies with respect when they realise that they may need them for longer.'

'I suppose,' I grumble.

Dr Oystein smiles. 'You will see the brighter side of your circumstances once you recover from the shock. But if it still troubles you, at least you have the comfort of knowing that you will not have to go through this alone. We are all in the same boat. We will support one another over the long decades to come.'

'All right,' I mutter and we start walking again. My mind's still whirling, but I try to put thoughts of my long future on hold and focus on the tour again. It's hard – I have a sick feeling in my stomach, like I get if I go too long without eating brains – but the doctor's right. I can obsess about this later. If I try to deal with it now, I'll go mad thinking about it. And madness is the last thing I want to face in my state. I mean, who fancies spending a couple of thousand years as a slack-jawed, drooling nutter!

FIVE

The tour draws to its conclusion shortly after our conversation in the corridor. We pass through one of the large courtyards of County Hall – I remember seeing them from up high when I went on the Eye in the past – and into a room which has been converted into a lab, lots of test tubes and vials, some odd-looking machines beeping away quietly in various places, pickled brains and other internal organs that have been set up for dissection and examination.

'This is not my main place of work,' Dr Oystein says. 'I maintain another laboratory elsewhere in the city. I had a string of similar establishments in different countries around the world, but I do not know what has become of them since the downfall.'

He looks at me seriously. 'I told you that we keep no secrets from one another here, and that is the truth, with one key exception. The other laboratory is where I conduct the majority of my experiments and tests, and where I keep the records of all that I have discovered over the years.'

'You mean you haven't just started researching zombies since the attacks?'

'No. I am over a hundred years old and have been studying the undead since the mid-1940s.' As I gawp at him, he continues as if what he's told me is no big deal. 'I have a team of scientists who have been working with me for many years. They are based at my main research centre. I lost a lot of good men and women when the city fell, but enough survived to assist me in my efforts going forward.

'I dare not reveal the location of that laboratory to anyone. It is not an issue of trust but of fear. There are dark forces stacked against us. You are aware of the one who calls himself Mr Dowling?'

'You know about the clown?' I gasp.

Dr Oystein nods sombrely. 'I will tell you more about him later. For now, know only that he is our enemy, the most dangerous foe we will ever face. He yearns for the complete destruction of mankind. I guard the secrets of deadly formulas that Mr Dowling could use to wipe out the living. If I told you where my laboratory was, and if he captured you and forced the information from you . . .'

I smile shakily. 'That's all right, doc. I know what a bastard he is. You don't need to feel bad about not sharing.'

'Yet I do,' he mutters glumly, then grimaces. 'Well, as

limited as this laboratory is, it does feature one of my more refreshing inventions, a device which is literally going to blow your mind. Come and see.'

Dr Oystein quickens his pace and leads me to four tall, glass-fronted cylinders near the rear of the lab. Each is about three metres high and one metre in diameter. One is filled with a dark grey liquid that looks like thick, gloopy soup.

'I have a complicated technical name for these,' Dr Oystein says. 'But one of my American Angels nicknamed them Groove Tubes some years ago and it stuck.'

'What are they for?' I ask.

'Recovery and recuperation.' The doctor pokes one of the deep gashes on my left arm and I wince. 'As you will have noticed, our bodies do not generate new cells to repair cuts and other wounds. Our only natural defence mechanism is the green moss which sprouts on open gashes. The moss prevents significant blood loss and holds strands of shredded flesh together, but it is not a curative aid. Broken bones don't mend. Cuts never properly close. Pain, once inflicted, must be endured indefinitely.'

'Tell me about it,' I huff, having been hunched over and limping since Trafalgar Square.

'We can endure the pain when we have to,' Dr Oystein continues, 'but it is a barrier. It is hard to focus when you are wracked with agony. Like you, I have suffered much in my time. I realised long ago that I needed to find some way to combat the pain, to ensure it did not distract me from my work. I conducted many experiments and eventually came up with the Groove Tube. In the fledgling world of zombie chemistry, this probably ranks as the most significant invention to date. If the undead awarded Nobel prizes . . .'

He smiles at the absurdity of the suggestion, then clears his throat. 'Although the technology is complicated, the results are easy to explain. The liquid inside a Groove Tube is a specially formulated solution which uses modified brain cells as its core ingredient. If you are undead and you immerse yourself, the solution stimulates some of the healing functions of your body.

'Your lesser wounds will heal inside the Tube. The cuts on your elbows and head will scab over, as they would have when you were alive. It won't have much of a visible effect on the hole in your chest, but it will patch up the worst damage and you will not bleed so freely.

'There are other benefits. Broken bones will mesh. Your eyesight will improve and your eyes will sting less. You will not need to use drops so often. You might get a few of your taste buds back, but that sensation won't last for long. You will come out feeling energetic and the pain will be far less than it currently is.'

'Sounds like a miracle cure,' I mutter, suspicious, as I always am, of anything that sounds too good to be true.

'A miracle, perhaps,' he says, 'but not a full-blown cure.

The effects are not permanent. If a bone has broken, the gel holding the two parts together will start to fail after a few years. All wounds will reopen in time. But you can immerse yourself again when that happens and be healed afresh. It is too soon to know if we can use the Tubes indefinitely, but so far I have not noticed any limit on the number of times that they can work their wonders on a given body.'

'Fair enough, doc. You've sold me.' I start to strip.

'One moment,' he stops me. 'I want you to be fully aware of what you are letting yourself in for.'

'I knew it,' I scowl. 'What's the catch?'

'We cannot sleep,' Dr Oystein says. 'Wakefulness is a curse of the undead and I have been unable to find a cure for it. But when we enter a Groove Tube, we hallucinate.'

'Go on,' I growl.

'It is like getting high,' the doctor murmurs, staring long-ingly at the grey gloop inside the cylinder. 'As the solution fills your lungs – you cannot drown, so it will not harm you, although we'll have to pump you dry when we pull you out – you will start to experience a sense of deep, overwhelming bliss. You will have visions and your brain will tune out the world beyond the Tube, as you enter a dreamlike state.'

'Sounds good to me,' I beam.

'It *is* good,' he nods. 'But there are dangers which you should be aware of. One is the addictive nature of the expe-rience. You will not want to leave. I could let my Angels soak in the Tubes regularly, but I do not. They are reserved for the treatment of serious wounds. The main reason I insist on that is to help them avoid becoming addicted. You may wish to re-enter the Tube at the end of the process, but I will not permit it. They are for medicinal – not recreational – purposes only.'

'Understood. And the real kicker?'

Dr Oystein nods. 'You are sharper than most of my Angels, B. Yes, I have held back the real kicker, as you call it, until the end.' He pauses. 'It will take two or three weeks for your wounds to fully heal. During that time you will be unaware of all that is happening around you. It would be a simple thing for me or anyone else to attack you while you are in that suspended state. You will have no way of defending yourself. If someone wanted to cut your head open and pulp your brain, it would be child's play. Or we could just leave you inside the Tube and never pull you out — if we did not haul you clear, you would bob up and down inside the solution for the rest of your existence, never fully waking. Once you succumb to the allure of the Groove Tube, you will be at our mercy.'

I stare at the doctor long and hard. 'That's a pretty big ask, doc.'

'Yes,' he says.

'Can I wait to make my decision?'

'Of course.'

'Will anything bad happen to me if I choose not to enter the Tube?' I watch him warily for his answer, ready to bolt for freedom if I get the feeling that he's spinning me a lie.

'If you mean will your wounds worsen, no. You will have to endure the pain, but that is all.'

I nod slowly, thinking it over. Then I decide to hell with it. Maybe I'm a fool, but I want to trust this guy. I *need* to trust him. I've felt so alone since I came back from the dead, even when I've been surrounded by others. Without someone to believe in, what's the point of going on?

'All right, doc,' I sigh as I take off the rest of my clothes. 'I can't be bothered waiting. I'm hopping in. You might have to adjust the temperature for me though — I like my bath-water *hot*.'

SIX

GgggggggggROOOOOOOOveeeeeeeeee!!!!!!!

SEVEN

Next thing I know, I'm flopping about on the floor of the lab like a dying fish, vomiting up liquid. The room seems extraordinarily bright. I moan and start to shield my eyes with a hand. Before I can, someone tosses a towel over my head and says something. I can't hear them clearly, so I slide my hand in under the towel to stick a finger in my ear and clear it out.

'No!' comes a roar loud enough to penetrate even my clogged ear canals. 'You might damage your ear with the bone sticking out of your finger.'

I'd forgotten about the bones. Lowering the hand, I try to ask the person their name, but my throat and mouth are full of the solution from the Tube.

'Keep as still as you can,' a boy says. 'We know what we're doing.'

Someone lifts the towel and gently runs a cotton bud

round the inside of my left ear, then my right. A plastic tube slides up under my chin and I'm instructed to feed it down my throat.

'I know it's gross,' a girl says, 'but we have to pump your stomach dry, otherwise you won't be able to talk.'

With a grimace, I stick the tube into my mouth – it's tricky because my teeth sprouted while I was blissed out – and force it down. When it can't play out any more, I hold it in place while a machine is switched on, and keep my lips open wide while liquid is pumped out of my stomach.

After several minutes there's nothing left to come up. The machine is turned off and I'm handed a pair of sunglasses.

'Put them on,' the girl tells me. 'The room will still seem brighter than normal, but you'll soon adjust.'

I slip on the shades and tug the towel from my head. Squinting against the light, I spot the boy and girl, both a bit younger than me.

'*Groo gar goo?*' I gurgle.

'Take it easy,' the boy says, picking up a smaller hooked tube. 'Your lungs are still full. We have to slide this down into them. Are you ready?'

'*Ghursh.*'

'I'll take that as a yes,' he smirks and carefully slides the tube into my mouth. He has a torch attached to a headband, the sort that surgeons use, and he shines it between my teeth as he searches for the correct opening. When he finds it, he begins to poke the tube down my windpipe. It's a horrible feeling and my instinct is to grind my teeth together and snap through the tube. But I know these guys are trying to help, so I fight the urges of my body.

The boy switches on the machine again and pumps my lungs dry. When he turns it off and withdraws the tube, I cough and scowl at the pair.

'Ish that iht?' I mumble, words still coming out garbled because of my oversized teeth, but a lot clearer than before.

'Just about,' the girl giggles. 'But the pump doesn't force out every last drop. The liquid will have made its way through your digestive system. We need to give you an enema.'

'What'sh that?' I ask.

She holds up a third tube. 'We need to insert this up your . . .' She nods at my bum.

'Ihf you try to shtick that fhing ihn me, I'll ram iht up *your* hole!' I bark, slapping the tube from her hands.

'Fine,' she shrugs. 'You can wear a nappy for the next week instead.'

I swear and glare at the grinning pair. 'Mahke him turn his bahck,' I growl.

'Like it's something I *want* to see,' the boy snorts and turns away, focusing his attention elsewhere.

I've never had an enema before, and I don't ever want one again, and that's all I'm saying about that!

When the girl has cleared me out, she leads me to a shower and I hose myself down, washing off the grey gunk from the Groove Tube. When I step out, she hands me a robe. I pull it on gratefully. Even though I'm cleaner than I've ever been, I feel strangely soiled.

'No need to be ashamed,' the girl says as I towel my hair dry. 'We all have to suffer this when we come out of the Groove Tubes. It's a small price to pay. Look at your arms.'

I roll up the sleeves of the robe and study my elbows. When I slid into the Tube, the flesh around them had been ripped to pieces, the bone exposed in places. Now they look almost as good as new. Scarred, pink flesh, but whole and healthy-looking.

I part the front of my robe and examine the hole in the left side of my chest. It's still an ugly, gaping wound, but it doesn't look as messy as it did. Some of the green moss has come away in the tank, and it's not as foresty as it was.

I close my robe again and stare at the glass-fronted cylinder. The liquid is being drained from it, but slowly. It's murkier than before, having absorbed dead cells, blood and all sorts of gunk from my body while I was bobbing up and down inside. I showered thoroughly before getting in, however many weeks ago it was, but there was still a lot of dirt to come out.

'Where'sh Docktohr Oyshteeen?' I ask.

'He's not here,' the boy says. 'He's been gone the last week or more, at his other laboratory. He told us to apologise on his behalf. He would have liked to be here to welcome you back into the world, but his work called him away.'

'It often does,' the girl says, 'so don't take it personally.'

'I whon't. Who are yhou?'

'I'm Cian,' the boy says.

'And I'm Awnya,' the girl adds. 'We're twins.'

'The only twin revitaliseds in London as far as we know,' Cian says proudly.

'Probably the world,' Awnya beams.

'Congrachulayshuns,' I mutter sarcastically.

'We're in charge of clothing, bedding, furniture and so on,' Cian tells me. 'If there's anything you need that you can't be bothered going to look for yourself, let us know and we'll do our best to get it for you, whether it's designer clothes, a certain brand of shoe or a specific type of hat.'

'We got rid of your old clothes,' Awnya says, 'but we held on to the slouch hat in case it had sentimental value. You'll find it on a shelf in your bedroom.'

'Thanksh.'

My gaze returns to the Groove Tube, longingly this time. I don't remember much after Dr Oystein helped me climb inside. I recall the feeling of the liquid oozing down my throat – surprisingly not as unpleasant as when I had to force it back up – but then I drifted off into a blissful state where everything seemed warm and right. It was like I used to feel when I'd lie in bed on a Sunday morning, having stayed up late to watch horror movies the night before, not asleep but not yet fully awake. The feeling of being somewhere comfortable and safe, the world not totally real, still part dreamy.

I smoked a bit of weed back in the day – Mum would have killed me if she'd known! – but I didn't try anything more exotic. Based on what friends of mine who had done harder drugs told me, the feeling I had inside the Groove Tube must have been a lot like going on a headtrip. Part of me wants to crawl back inside and bliss out again, return to the land of dreams and stay there forever, escape this world of the living dead. But I recall what Dr Oystein told me about only using the Tubes to cure injuries. Besides, that would be like committing suicide. This is a bad, mad world, but running away from it isn't the answer. Well, it's not *my* answer.

I'm about to ask the twins to show me to my room when I glance at the other Groove Tubes and come to a halt. One of the Tubes is occupied by a large teenager. He has a big head, hair cut close, small ears, beady eyes. Fat, rosy cheeks, a chunk bitten out of the left one. He looks like a real bruiser, and I know that in this case looks are definitely *not* deceptive.

The last time I saw this guy was in a corridor deep underground. He'd just killed a scientist and scooped the still-warm brain from the dead man's skull. He was a zom head like me and the others, but he took off solo, leaving the rest of us to rot. He cared only for himself and was prepared to kill his guardians and betray his friends as long as it suited his own selfish purposes.

He looks comical, floating in the Tube, naked, eyes open as they are on all zombies, but expression distant. He's unaware of everything, defenceless, at the mercy of Dr Oystein and his Angels.

And me.

But I'm not prepared to show him mercy, just as he didn't show any to me, Mark or the other zom heads. This bastard deserves execution more than most, and I'm just the girl to do the world that small favour.

'*Rhage!*' I snarl, pressing my face up close to the glass of the Groove Tube. Then I step back and look around eagerly for a weapon to kill him.

EIGHT

'No, B,' Cian snaps and tries to pull me back.

I wrestle with the boy and throw him to the floor. Awnya rushes me, but I grab her by the throat, then slam her to the ground beside her brother. Good to see the old fighting touch hasn't deserted me.

The twins quickly and easily dealt with, I turn back towards the Groove Tube, fingers flexing, snarling viciously. But before I can focus, someone says, 'Take one more step towards him and I'll fry you.'

I pause and peer around the lab. At first I can't see anyone. Then he moves and I spot him, standing close to the door which opens on to the courtyard. He takes several strides towards me and his face swims into view. A burly man with brown hair and stubble, wearing a dark blue outfit that wouldn't look out of place on a security guard. The last time I saw him, he was in military fatigues.

'*Rheilly?*' I gawp.

The soldier smiles tightly. 'None other.'

'What the hell are yhou doing here?'

'The same as usual — guarding those who don't deserve guarding.'

Reilly stops a couple of metres from me. He's holding some sort of a gun, but it doesn't look like any I've seen before.

'Step away from the Tube, B.'

'Shkroo yhou, arsh hohl,' I snap.

His smile broadens. 'That was one of the first things you said when we originally filed your teeth down, back when you revitalised. It's like we've come full circle. I feel nostalgic.'

'Fhunny guy,' I sneer, than tap the glass of the Groove Tube. 'He killed Docktohr Sherverus.'

'I know.'

'Pohked his eye out, cut his head open and tuhcked in.'

'I'm not a goldfish,' Reilly sniffs. 'I was there. I remember.'

'Sho I'm gonna kill him. Retchribooshun.'

'Don't make me laugh,' Reilly snorts. 'You hated Dr Cerveris. His death didn't matter to you in the slightest.'

I shake my head. 'Yesh, I hated him. But I didn't whant to kill him. Rhage ish a shavage. Becaush ohf him, Mark and the othersh are dead.'

'I know,' Reilly says, softly this time. 'That sucks, the way they slaughtered the revitaliseds. It's one of the reasons I cut my ties with Josh and the rest after they'd regained control of the complex. But Dr Oystein offered Rage a home when he came here, wounded like you were, in need of sanctuary, even though he wouldn't admit it. Rage was dubious, especially when he saw you. He wanted to kill you, like you want to kill him. But Dr Oystein protected you and promised to do the same for Rage while he was incapable of defending himself.'

'Don't care,' I growl. 'Gonna kill him anywhay.'

Reilly raises his gun.

'Don't tell me it'sh me ohr him,' I groan.

'No,' Reilly says. 'I'm not going to kill you. This is a stun gun. It fires spiked electrodes into your flesh, then fries you with a burst of electricity that would bring down an elephant. You're tough, B, but this will floor you for at least half an hour. Trust me, you do *not* want to put yourself through that. However bad your enema felt, it's nothing in comparison with this.'

'Yhou were whatching that?' I snarl.

'Don't worry,' he grins. 'I averted my gaze during the more sensitive moments. I've visited the great pyramids, Petra, the temples of Angkor Wat. Your bunghole doesn't rank high on my list of must-sees.'

I laugh despite myself. 'Yhou're a bashtard, Rheilly.'

'Takes one to know one,' he retorts. 'Now step away

from the Tube and let the twins escort you to your quarters.'

'What ihf I shay shkroo the quahrters? What ihf I don't whant anything to do with idiotsh who give shelter to a monshter like him?'

Reilly shrugs. 'You need the Angels a lot more than they need you. Dr Oystein will be sad if you reject his offer of hospitality, but as for the rest of us, nobody will miss you.'

I come close to leaving. I'm on the verge of telling Reilly that he can marry Rage if he loves him that much. Then Awnya steps up beside me and shakes her head.

'Don't do it, B. It's horrible out there. Cian and I were lucky — we had each other. But we were lonely until we came here. And scared.'

'We saw terrible things,' Cian murmurs. 'We *did* terrible things.' He pulls his jumper aside to reveal a deep, moss-encrusted bite mark on his shoulder. 'We became monsters when we turned. Dr Oystein doesn't care. He gave us a home, and he'll give you one too if you let him.'

'But thish guy ish a bruhte!' I yell. 'He'sh not like ush. He killed when he didn't need to and kept the brain for himshelf.'

'Are you pissed because he didn't share Dr Cerveris's brain with you?' Reilly chuckles.

'No,' I sneer. 'I'm pisshed becaush Mark was killed. Ihf Rhage had let the resht of ush eat, the othersh wouldn't have needed to kill Mark. Maybe Josh would have shpared them too.'

'I doubt it,' Reilly says. 'I wasn't privy to the decisions that were made that day, but I think all of the zom heads were scheduled for execution once it became clear that we had to evacuate. They didn't dare let you guys run wild. I don't know why Josh let you go, but the others would have been eliminated no matter what.'

'Maybe,' I concede. 'That doeshn't change the fact that Rhage did whrong.'

'No,' Reilly agrees. 'It doesn't. But it's part of my job now to look after those who need help, regardless of anything they did or didn't do in the past. I might not like it – in fact forget about *might*, I *don't* – but we're playing by Dr Oystein's rules here. Maybe he sees potential for good in Rage that you or I missed. Or maybe he's taking a gamble and will come to view him as the sly, turncoat killer that we both know and loathe. If he does, and he asks me to handle the situation, I'll be only too delighted to pay back Rage for what he did to Cerveris and the others, but –'

'Othersh?' I interrupt.

'Cerveris wasn't the only one he killed while he was breaking out,' Reilly says. 'I didn't have many friends in that place, but he murdered a couple of guys I knew who were good men, just trying to do their job. I've no sympathy for him.'

'Then why don't you help me shettle the shcore?' I whine.

'Because I trust Dr Oystein,' Reilly says simply. 'I trust his judgement even more than my own. I've only known him for a month and a bit, so maybe that's a crazy claim, but it's how I feel. I went along with orders underground because that was what I'd always done. Everything had gone to hell and I thought the only way to deal with the madness was to carry on as if it was business as usual.

'But I'm cooperating with Dr Oystein because I truly believe that he can lead the living out of this mess, that he can help those of us who survived to find a better way forward. If he says that Rage has the same rights as the rest of the revitaliseds, who am I to question him?'

I swear bitterly, knowing I can't win this argument. My choice is clear — walk away and return to the chaos and loneliness of the undead city beyond these walls, or play along and see what Dr Oystein has to say for himself when he returns.

'Thish ishn't ohver,' I tell Reilly. 'Rhage and I have unfhinished bishness.'

'Sure you do,' Reilly laughs. 'Just don't try to sort it out while I'm guarding him — if we got into a fight and you scratched me, you'd turn me into a revived, and I don't think either of us wants that, do we?'

'Don't be sho shure about that,' I jeer, showing him my fangs, but it's an idle threat. I'd hate to have his blood on my hands.

I give Reilly a long, slow stare. Then Cian and Awnya drag me out of the lab. I leave reluctantly, finding it hard to tear my gaze away from Reilly and the devious, deceitful creep bobbing up and down inside the grey, clammy solution of the Groove Tube.

NINE

I scowl and mutter to myself as I stomp through the courtyard. Cian and Awnya have to jog to keep up.

'You really like that guy then?' Cian jokes.

'He abahndhoned me and my fhriends,' I growl. 'Lehft
ush to be killed. Called ush a bunch of looshers. He'sh
shkum.'

'Dr Oystein will be able to help him,' Awnya says confidently.

'He doeshn't need help,' I sneer. 'He needsh execy-
ooshun.'

I shake my head, sigh and slow down. We're still in the
courtyard. I look up at the sky. It's a cloudy, grey day, I'm
guessing late morning or early afternoon.

'Here,' Cian says, handing me a small metal file. I think it's
one of the ones I was carrying when I arrived. 'I was going

to give you this in your room, but maybe you'd prefer it now.'

'Thanksh.' I set to work on my teeth – it's tricky without a mirror – and grind away at those which have sprouted the most. The twins wait patiently, saying nothing as bits of enamel go flying across the yard. When I feel halfway normal, I lower the file, run my tongue around my teeth and say my name and old address out loud. I'm still not perfect, but a lot better than I was before.

'How long was I in the Groove Tube?' I ask.

'Just over three weeks,' Awnya says.

'Twenty-four days,' Cian elaborates.

'*Twenty-four Days Later*,' I say sombrely, deepening my voice to sound like a movie announcer. The twins stare at me blankly. 'You know, like *Twenty-eight Days Later*?' They haven't a clue what I'm talking about. 'Didn't you watch zombie movies before all this happened?'

'No,' Awnya says. 'They scared me.'

'And we always watched movies together,' Cian says. 'So if one of us didn't like a certain type of film, the other couldn't watch it either.'

'That's why I never got to see any chick flicks,' Awnya says, shooting her twin a dark look.

'Life's too short,' Cian snorts. 'Even if we live to be three thousand, it will still be too short as far as chick flicks are concerned.'

'Well, I won't let you watch any zombie movies either,' Awnya pouts.

'Like I want to watch any now,' Cian laughs.

I study the twins. They're about the same height. Both have blond hair and fair skin. They look similar and are dressed in matching, cream-coloured clothes. A chunk has been bitten out of Awnya's left hand, just above her little finger. I see bone shining through the green, wispy moss. In the daylight they look even younger than they did in the lab, no more than twelve or thirteen.

'Were you guys attacked at the same time?' I ask.

'Yeah,' Cian says.

'But I got bitten first,' Awnya says. 'He could have escaped but he came back for me. The idiot.'

'I wouldn't have bothered if I'd known you were going to tuck into me,' Cian sniffs, rubbing his shoulder through the fabric of his jumper.

'She turned on you?' I smirk wickedly.

'It wasn't her fault,' Cian says, quick to defend his sister. 'She didn't know what she was doing. None of us did when we were in that state. At least she didn't rip my skull open, or that would have been the real end of me.'

'Your nasty brain would have turned my stomach,' Awnya says and the twins beam at each other.

'Nice to see you don't bear a grudge,' I note.

Cian shrugs. 'What's done is done. Besides, this way we

can carry on together. I wouldn't have wanted to escape and live normally if it meant leaving Awnya behind. I'd rather be a zombie with her than a human on my own.'

'Pass me the sick bag,' I groan, but grin to let them know I'm only joking.

It starts to rain, so we step inside and the twins lead me to my bedroom.

'How long have you guys been here?' I ask.

'Ages,' Awnya yawns. 'We revitalised quickly, less than a week after we were turned.'

'We were among the first to recover their senses,' Cian boasts. 'Dr Oystein says we're two of his most incredible Angels.'

I frown. 'This place was open for business that soon after the attacks?'

'No,' Awnya says. 'We wandered for a couple of weeks before we noticed the arrows.'

'That was a scary time,' Cian says softly and the pair link hands.

'Dr Oystein was based in Hyde Park when we found him,' Awnya continues. 'He put up a tent in the middle of the park and that's where his first Angels joined him and sheltered. He was already working on modifying this place, but it was another few weeks before we were able to move in.'

'Did he have Groove Tubes in Hyde Park?'

'He had one,' Cian says, 'but it was no good. There was a

generator to power it, but the noise attracted reviveds. They kept attacking and knocking it out — they didn't like the sound. He wasn't able to mount a proper guard, so in the end he left it until we moved here.'

'A couple of revitaliseds died because of that,' Awnya says sadly. 'They were so badly wounded, in so much pain, that they killed themselves.'

'I've never seen Dr Oystein look so miserable,' Cian croaks. 'If he could cry, I think he'd still be weeping now.'

There's a long silence, broken only by the sound of our footsteps.

'How did you end up doing this?' I ask. 'Taking people round and getting stuff for them?'

'We're good at it,' Awnya smiles. 'Dr Oystein says we're like jackdaws — we can find a pearl anywhere.'

'Our mum was a shopaholic,' Cian says. 'She dragged us everywhere with her. We got to be pretty good at finding our way round stores and tracking down items that she was interested in. When Dr Oystein saw how quickly we could secure materials, he put us in charge of supplies. It didn't matter that we're two of the youngest Angels. He said we were the best people for the job.'

'Of course he was probably concerned about us too,' Awnya says. 'Being so young, I think he was worried that we might not be as capable as the others, and he wanted to find something to keep us busy, so we didn't feel out of place.'

'No way,' Cian barks. 'I keep telling you that's not the case. We train with the other guys and hold our own. Dr Oystein could send us on missions if he wanted. We just happen to be better than anyone else at doing this.'

Awnya catches my eye and we share a secret smile. Boys always want to think that they're able to do anything. We usually let them enjoy their fantasies. They're happier that way and do less whining.

'What sort of missions do the others go on?' I ask.

'Dull stuff mostly,' Cian huffs, and I decide to leave it there for the time being, as it's obviously a sore point for him.

We come to a closed door and Cian pushes it open. We step into one of County Hall's many huge rooms. There are six single beds arranged in a circle in the centre. The sheets and pillows on four of them have the crumpled look that shows they've been used recently. The other two have perfectly folded sheets and crease-free pillowcases.

There are three wardrobes, lots of shelving and two long dressing tables, one on either side of the room, with mirrors hanging on the walls above them, stools set underneath.

A girl is sitting on one of the stools, my age if not a bit older. She looks like an Arab, light brown skin, a plain blue robe and white headscarf. She's working on a model of the

Houses of Parliament, made out of matchsticks. It looks pretty damn cool.

'Oh, hi, Ashtat,' Awnya says. 'We didn't know you were here.'

The girl half waves at us without looking round.

'This is Becky, but she prefers B,' Awnya presses on.

'Hush,' Ashtat murmurs.

'What's your problem?' I growl.

Ashtat scowls at me. 'I do not like being interrupted when I'm working on my models. You cannot know that, never having met me before, but the twins do. They should not have admitted you until I was finished.'

'Like Awnya said, we didn't know you were here,' Cian protests. 'We thought you'd still be training with the others.'

'I tired of training early today,' Ashtat sniffs.

'Well, I'm here, so you'll have to live with it,' I tell her, determined to make my mark from the start. If I let her treat me like a dog now, I'll have to put up with that all the way down the line.

Ashtat raises an eyebrow but says nothing and returns to her model, carefully gluing another matchstick into place.

'She's OK when she's not working on a model,' Awnya whispers. 'Let's come back later.'

'No,' I say out loud. 'I'm staying. If she doesn't like that, tough. Which bed is mine?'

Awnya shows me to one of the spare beds. There's a

bedside cabinet next to it. A few files for my teeth rest on top of the cabinet, along with the watches I was wearing, one of which was smashed to pieces in Trafalgar Square.

'Your hat's over there,' Cian says, pointing to a shelf. The shelf is blue, and so are the two shelves above it. 'The blue shelves are yours. You can stick anything you want on them, clothes, books, CDs, whatever. Half of that wardrobe –' he points to my left, '– is yours too. You're sharing with a guy called Jakob. He doesn't have much, so you should have plenty of room.'

'What about a bedroom of my own?' I ask.

Cian and Awnya shake their heads at the same time, the exact same way.

'Dr Oystein says it's important for us to share,' Cian says.

'It's the same for every Angel,' Awnya says. 'Nobody gets their own room.'

I frown. 'That's weird, isn't it?'

'It's meant to bring us closer together,' Awnya says.

'Plus it stops people arguing about who gets the rooms with the best views and most space,' Cian says.

'All right,' I sniff. 'I don't suppose I'll be using it much anyway. It's not like we need to sleep, is it?'

'No,' Cian says hesitantly. 'But Dr Oystein prefers it if we keep regular hours. We act as we did when we were alive. Most of us get up about seven every morning, do our chores, train, hang out, eat, whatever. Then we come to bed at mid-night and lie in the dark for seven hours, resting.'

'It's good to have a routine,' Awnya says. 'It's comforting. You don't have to use your bed – nobody's going to force you – but if you want to fit in with the rest of us ...'

'Sounds worse than prison,' I grumble, but I'm com-plaining just for the sake of it. Sinking on to the bed, I pick at my robe. 'What about clothes?'

'We thought you might want to choose your own,' Awnya says. 'We can get gear for you if you have specific requests. Otherwise we'll take you out later and show you round some of our favourite shops.'

'That sounds good,' I smile. 'I like to pick my own stuff.'

'We figured as much,' Awnya says smugly. 'We'll come and collect you in an hour or so.'

'What will I do until then?' I ask.

The twins shrug in unison.

'Get the feel of the place,' Cian says.

'Relax,' Awnya suggests.

'Keep quiet,' Ashtat lobs in.

I give her the finger, even though she can't see me, and slip on the watch that works, an ultra-expensive model that I picked up in the course of my travels. As the twins leave, I start to ask them for the correct time, in case the watch is wrong, but they're gone before I can.

I sigh and stare around the room, at the bed, the furniture, the silent girl and her matchstick model. Then, because I've nothing better to do, and because I'm a wicked sod, I start filing my teeth again, as loudly as I can, treating myself to a mischievous grin every time Ashtat twitches and shoots me a dirty look.

TEN

The twins take me over the river and into the Covent Garden area. True to their word, they know all the best shops, not just those with the coolest gear, but those with the least zombies. The living dead don't bother us much once they realise we're like them, but it's still easier to browse in places where they aren't packed in like sardines.

I choose several pairs of black jeans, a variety of dark T-shirts, a few jumpers and a couple of jackets. New sunglasses too, and a baseball cap with a skull design that I spot in a window, for those days when I don't feel like the Australian hat which has served me well so far.

When it comes to shoes, the twins have a neat little device which screws into the material, making holes for the bones sticking out of my toes to jut through. They measure my feet and bore the holes with all the care of professional cobblers.

'I like it,' I grunt, admiring my new trainers.

'Dr Oystein invented that years ago,' Cian tells me, pocketing the gadget. 'He's like one of those crazy inventors you read about in comics.'

'Only not actually crazy,' Awnya adds.

'I don't know about –' I start to say, but a rapping sound on the shop window stops me.

We all instantly drop to our knees. There's another rap, a loud, clattering sound, but I can't see anyone.

'Do you think it's a revived?' I whisper.

'I don't know,' Cian says.

'I hope so,' Awnya croaks.

There's a long silence. I look around for another way out. Then there are two more raps on the glass. I spot a hand, low down and to the left, close to the open door. Another two raps. Then a series of short raps.

I roll my eyes and stand. 'Very funny,' I shout.

'Careful, B,' Awnya moans. 'We don't know who it is.'

'But we know they have lousy taste in movies,' I snort. 'I recognise those raps. They're the theme tune from *Jaws*.'

'And what's wrong with that?' a girl challenges me, stepping into view outside. '*Jaws* is a classic.'

'The hell it is,' I reply. 'A boring old film with lousy special effects, and hardly anyone gets killed.'

'You don't know what you're talking about,' the girl says, stepping into the shop. Four teenage boys appear and follow her in. The girl smiles at the twins. 'Hey, guys, sorry if we frightened you.'

'We weren't frightened,' Cian says with a dismissive shake of his head, as if the very idea is offensive to him. 'We were excited. Thought we were going to see some action at last.'

'This is Ingrid,' Awnya introduces the girl. 'She's one of us.'

'I figured as much.' I cast an eye over the tall, blonde, athletic-looking girl. She's dressed in leathers, a bit like those the zom heads used to wear when they were tormenting reviveds.

'You must be B,' Ingrid says.

'Word travels fast,' I smile.

'Not that fast,' Ingrid says. 'You were in a Groove Tube for almost a month.'

My smile vanishes.

'What are you doing over here?' Cian asks. 'Are you on a mission?'

'Yeah,' Ingrid says.

'What sort of a mission?' I ask.

'The usual,' she shrugs. 'Looking for survivors. Searching for brains. Keeping an eye out for Mr Dowling or any other intruders.'

'We do this a lot,' one of the boys says. 'Not the most interesting of jobs, but it gets us out of County Hall.'

'Sounds like fun,' I lie, eager to see what they get up to. 'Can I come with you?'

'Absolutely not,' Ingrid says. 'You haven't been cleared for action by Master Zhang.'

'Aw, go on, Ingrid,' Cian pleads. 'If it's a normal mission, where's the harm? We can tag along too. We won't tell.'

'I don't know,' Ingrid says. 'This is serious business. If anything happened to you . . .'

'It won't,' Awnya says, as keen as her brother to get involved.

Ingrid checks with the rest of her pack. 'What do you guys think?'

They shrug. 'Doesn't matter to us,' one of them says.

'Three mugs to throw to Mr Dowling and his mutants if they turn up,' another guy smiles. 'Might buy us enough time to slip away.'

'Bite me,' I snap, and they all laugh.

'OK,' Ingrid decides. 'You can keep us company for a while. The experience will be good for you. But don't get in our way, do what we tell you and run like hell if we get into trouble.'

'How will we know?' Awnya asks nervously.

'Oh, trouble's easy to spot,' Ingrid says with an icy smile. 'It'll be when people start dying.'

ELEVEN

The Angels check the apartments above the shops, searching for survivors who might be holed up, or the corpses of people who died recently, whose brains might still be edible. They don't talk much, operating in silence most of the time, sweeping the rooms swiftly and efficiently.

One of the guys opens all of the doors. He has a set of skeleton keys and can deal with just about any lock that he encounters.

'That's Ivor Bolton,' Awnya whispers.

'Was he a thief when he was alive?' I ask.

'No. Master Zhang taught him.'

'Who's that?'

'Our mentor,' Awnya says. 'He trains every Angel. You'll meet him soon.'

'Do you all learn how to open locks?' I ask.

'Only those who show a natural talent for it,' Cian says.

I stare at Ivor enviously. I hope I show that sort of promise. I'd love to be able to crack open locks and gain entrance to anywhere I wanted.

We explore more rooms, Ingrid and her team taking it slowly, carefully, searching for hiding places in wardrobes and under beds, tapping the walls for secret panels.

'Do you ever find people?' I ask as we exit a building and move on.

'Living people?' Ingrid shrugs. 'Rarely, around here. Most of the survivors in this area moved on or died ages ago. We dig up the occasional fresh corpse, but mainly we're checking that the buildings are clear, that potential enemies aren't setting up base close to County Hall.'

'What do you do if you find someone alive?' I ask.

She shrugs again. 'It depends on whether they want to come with us or not. Many don't trust us and leg it. If they stop and listen, we tell them about County Hall and offer to take them to it, and from there to somewhere safe.'

'That's one of the main things the Angels do,' Awnya chips in. 'We lead survivors out of London to secure camps in the countryside.'

'It's not as easy as it sounds,' Cian says.

'I bet not,' I grunt, thinking of all the difficulties I faced simply getting from the East End to here. 'Have you been on any of those missions yet?' I ask Ingrid.

'No,' she sighs. 'It's all been local scouting missions for us so far.'

'Long may they continue,' one of the boys mutters.

Cian scowls. 'You don't want to tackle the harder challenges?'

'We're not suicidal,' the boy snorts.

'Do you feel the same way?' I ask Ingrid.

She looks uncertain. 'Part of me wants to be a hero. But some of the Angels who go on the more dangerous missions don't make it back.'

We enter another building, a block of flats set behind a row of shops. We start up the stairs, the plan being to work our way down from the top. We're coming to the top of the fourth flight when Ingrid stops abruptly and presses herself against the wall.

'What's wrong?' I ask, as she makes some gestures to the boys in her team.

'I think I heard something,' she whispers.

'What?'

'I'm not sure. But we were here just a week ago. The place was deserted then.' She points to Ivor and another of the boys and sends them forward to check.

We wait in silence for the pair to return. I feel out of my depth. I want a weapon, something to defend myself with. Although, looking round at the others, I see that they don't have any weapons either. I want to ask them why they came out without knives or guns, but I don't want to be the one to break the silence.

There's no sign of Ivor and his partner. Ingrid gives it a few minutes, then signals to the other two boys to go and look for them.

'This is bad,' Cian groans quietly.

Ingrid fries him with a heated look and presses a finger to her lips.

The seconds tick away slowly. I keep checking the time on my watch. I want to push forward to find out what's happening, but I'm a novice here. I don't have the right to take control.

Ingrid waits a full five minutes, then swears mutely, just mouthing the word. She looks at me and the twins. Makes a gulping motion and licks her lips. Nods at us to backtrack and follows us down to the third floor.

'I don't know what's going on, but it can't be anything good,' she says quietly. 'Wait here for me, but no more than a couple of minutes. If I don't come back or shout to let you know that it's safe, return to County Hall and send others after us. *Do not* follow me up there, no matter what, OK?'

'I'm scared,' Awnya whimpers.

Cian hugs her, but he looks even more worried than his sister.

Ingrid casts a questioning glance at me.

'I'll take care of them,' I tell her.

She nods, then pads up the stairs.

Time seems to slow down even more. I fix my gaze on my watch, willing the hands to move faster, wanting Ingrid and her crew to appear and give us the all-clear. But when that doesn't happen, and the time limit passes, I look up at the twins.

'We're leaving?' Cian asks.

I shake my head. 'I can't. I've got to help them if I can. You guys go. Don't wait for me. Go now.'

'No,' Awnya says, horrified. 'Come with us, B. You can't go up there by yourself.'

'I have to. Don't argue. Get the hell out of here and tell the others what has happened.'

'But ...' She looks like she wants to cry, but being undead, she can't.

I start up as the twins start down. They go slowly, hesitantly, unable to believe that I'm following Ingrid and her team. I can barely believe it either. I must be mad. I hardly know them. I don't owe them anything. I should beat it with the twins.

But I don't. Maybe it's because I want to be a dumb hero. Or maybe it's because I don't think anything can be as scary as Mr Dowling and his mutants. Or maybe it's the memory of Tyler Bayor, and what I did to him, that drives me on. Whatever the reason, I climb the steps, readying myself for battle, wondering what can have taken the Angels

223

so swiftly and silently. I didn't even hear one of them squeak.

As I get to the top step and turn into the corridor, there's a sudden, piercing scream. It's Ingrid. I can't see her, but I hear her racing footsteps as she roars at me, 'Run, B, run!'

'Bloody hell!' I yell, and I'm off, tearing down the stairs like a rabbit, running for my life, panting as if I had lungs that worked.

I catch up with the twins. They're making sobbing sounds.

'What –' Awnya starts to ask.

'No questions,' I shout. 'Just run!'

We hit the ground floor in a frightened huddle and spill out on to the street. Our legs get tangled up and all three of us sprawl across the road. I curse loudly and push myself to my feet. I grab Awnya and pull her up. I'm reaching for Cian, to help him, when I hear . . .

. . . laughter overhead.

I pause, a familiar sickening feeling flooding my guts, and look up.

Ingrid and the boys are spread across the fourth-floor landing, and they're all laughing their heads off.

'Suckers!' Ivor bellows.

'Run, fools, run,' another of the boys cackles.

'Those sons of bitches,' I snarl.

'What's going on?' Cian asks, bewildered. 'Was it a joke?'

'Yeah,' I snap. 'And we fell for it.'

224

'Oh, thank God,' Awnya sighs. 'I thought they'd been killed.'

'Arseholes!' I roar at the five Angels on the landing, and give them the finger.

'You've got to be alert when you're out on a mission, B,' Ingrid cries. 'Wait. What's that behind us? No! Help us, B. Save us. There's a monster coming to . . .' She screams again, high-pitched and false.

'Yeah, laugh it up,' I shout. 'You won't be laughing when I stick my foot so far up your arse that . . .'

I shake my head, disgusted. But I'm disgusted at myself for falling for the trick, not at the Angels for pulling it. I should have known better.

'Come on,' I grunt at the twins. 'Let's leave them to their precious mission. We've better things to be doing back at County Hall.'

'That wasn't nice, Ingrid,' Awnya shouts.

'It was horrible,' Cian agrees.

'I know,' Ingrid says, looking contrite. Then she cackles again. 'But it was *fun*!'

We head off, pointedly ignoring those who made fools of us, but I stop when Ingrid calls to me.

'B!'

I turn stiffly, expecting another insult.

'All joking aside, we respect that you came back to try and help.'

'Yeah,' Ivor says. 'That took guts.'

'We'll be seeing you again soon on a mission, I think,' Ingrid says. 'But next time you'll be one of us, in on the joke, not the butt of it.'

'Whatever,' I sniff.

I carry on back towards County Hall with the twins, as if what Ingrid and Ivor said meant nothing to me, but it's a struggle to maintain my scowl and not smile with stupid pride all the way.

TWELVE

We head back over the river. We can laugh about what happened in the building by the time we've crossed the bridge.

'We've got to play a joke on them now,' Cian says. 'Not straight away, but within the next day or two. I'll think of something good. Maybe make them believe we're being attacked in the middle of the night, so that they panic and rush outside.'

There's a strange buzzing in the air as we step off the bridge and start towards County Hall. 'What's that?' I ask, grimacing as I draw to a halt.

'The speakers,' Awnya says. 'There are lots of them positioned around the area, to stop reviveds coming too close. They play this high-pitched noise all the time.'

'We'll slip past them as we get closer to the building,' Cian says. 'The speakers all point away from it, so we'll be fine once we're through.'

'How come I didn't hear it before?' I ask.

'Most of them have a small button that you can press to temporarily disable them,' Awnya says. 'I did that as we were leaving.'

'I didn't notice.'

Awnya shrugs. 'No reason why you should have.'

The twins show me the speakers as we get closer, and show me how to turn them off if I'm ever passing by myself. Then we head on into the building. They take me to my bedroom – I'm still not sure of the layout of the building, and where everything is – and I lay my gear on the shelves. There's no sign of Ashtat or any of the others.

The twins go off on their own for a while, leaving me to sort through my stuff and rest. Then they return and guide me to a dining room, close to the kitchen that I passed through earlier. Circular tables dot the room and groups of teenagers are clustered round them, chatting noisily. I do a quick count — there are just over thirty Angels.

'That's yours,' Awnya says, pointing at a table of three boys and Ashtat.

'Are those my room-mates?'

'Yes.'

'What are they like?'

Awnya shrugs. 'Ashtat can be moody, like you saw, but she's not so bad. Carl and Shane are OK. Jakob doesn't say much.'

'Which one's he?' I ask.

'The thin, bald one.'

'Carl's the dark-haired one,' Cian adds. 'Shane's the ginger.'

I wince, recalling the fate of the last redhead I knew, poor Tiberius.

'Go on over,' Awnya says. 'You don't want to eat with us. It'll look strange if you avoid them.'

I nod. 'Thanks for showing me around today.'

'That's our job,' Cian smirks.

'All part of the service,' Awnya grins.

They slip away to their own table and I stare at the teenagers seated at mine. Carl's dressed in designer gear, real flash. Shane's wearing a tracksuit, but with a gold chain dangling from his neck, like a wannabe rapper. Jakob is wearing a white shirt and dark trousers which look about two sizes too big for him. He's one of the unhealthiest-looking people I've ever seen, even by zombie standards. If I didn't know he was already dead, I'd swear he was at death's door.

And then there's Ashtat, dressed as she was when I saw her earlier. She spots me and says something to the others. They look at me curiously. I feel nervous, like I did on my first day of school.

'Sod it,' I mutter. 'They've got more reason to be scared of me than I have to be scared of them. I'm badass B Smith, and don't you forget it!'

With a scowl and a disinterested sniff, I cross the great expanse of the dining room, walking big, trying to act as if I belong.

'All right?' I grunt as I take a seat at the table.

Everyone nods but nobody says anything.

'I'm B.'

'We know,' Carl says, checking out my clothes. He nods again. I think I have his approval on the fashion front.

'Have the twins been taking care of you?' Shane asks.

'Yeah.'

'They're good at that.'

'Yeah.' There's an uncomfortable silence. Then I decide to wade straight in. 'Look, I don't like being told who my friends are. If it was up to me, I'd mix with the others, chat with different people, make up my own mind who I like and who I don't. I've already met Ingrid and her team, and I'd be happy to hang out with them. But I've been stuck with you lot for the time being, so we're just going to have to live with it.'

Carl laughs. 'You were never taught how to make a good first impression, were you?'

I shrug. 'This is me. I won't pretend to be something I'm not.'

'And what are you exactly?' Ashtat asks quietly.

'That's for you to work out,' I tell her, meeting her gaze and not looking away.

'We've got a live one here,' Shane chuckles.

'So to speak,' Carl adds, then sticks out a hand. 'Carl Clay. Kensington born and bred.'

'I was wondering about the posh accent,' I say as we shake hands.

'You should hear it when I'm trying to impress,' he grins.

I haven't had much contact with people like Carl. Kids from Kensington didn't wander over east too much in my day, unless to see some grungy art gallery or to go shopping in Canary Wharf. I don't like his accent, and I don't want to like him either, but his smile seems genuine. I'll give him a chance — just not much of one.

'Shane Fitz,' the ginger introduces himself. Shane doesn't offer to shake hands, just nods at me. I nod back. The chain-wearing Shane's the sort of bloke I'd have kicked the crap out of if our paths had crossed in the past. But times have changed. We're in the same boat now. As with Carl, I'll wait to pass judgement, see what he's made of.

'Ashtat Kiarostami,' the girl says softly, tilting her head. 'I would like to apologise if I was rude to you earlier. I don't like to be disturbed when I'm working on my models and sometimes I react more sharply than intended.'

'Don't worry about it,' I sniff and look to the last of the four, the thin, bald kid with dark circles under his eyes.

'Jakob Pegg,' he wheezes and that's all I get out of him.

'So what's your story?' Carl asks, settling back in his chair.

'Where are you from? How were you killed? When did you revitalise?'

I tell them a bit about myself, the East End, the attack on my school, regaining consciousness in the underground complex. They're intrigued by that and pump me for more information. They haven't heard of anything like it before.

'I bet Dr Oystein was furious when you told him about that place,' Shane remarks.

'He knew about it already,' I reply. 'He said he had contacts there.'

Shane frowns. 'It can't have been anything to do with Dr Oystein. He wouldn't approve of revitaliseds being imprisoned and experimented on.'

'Dr Oystein's approval doesn't mean much to the army,' Carl snorts. 'They do what they like. He has to keep them onside or they'll target us.'

'Bring 'em on,' Shane growls.

'Don't be stupid,' Ashtat chides him. 'They could level this place from the air. We would not even see who killed us.'

'So how'd you get out of there?' Carl asks as Shane seethes at the injustice of the world.

'Ever hear of a guy called Mr Dowling?'

Carl's eyes widen and Ashtat shivers. Shane pulls back from me, while Jakob leans forward, looking interested for the first time.

'I'll take that as a yes,' I say drily.

'We have heard rumours,' Ashtat murmurs, shivering again. 'Terrible rumours. If we could sleep, we would all have nightmares about him.'

'Speak for yourself,' Shane snorts, but he looks uneasy.

I tell them how the crazed clown and his mutants invaded the complex and slaughtered many of the staff. But they didn't harm me or any of the other zom heads. Mr Dowling freaked me out – I wince as I recount how he opened his mouth and spat a stream of live spiders into my face – but he set me free once he'd made me tremble and shriek.

'I don't get it,' Shane frowns. 'Why did he free you? I thought Mr Dowling was our enemy.'

'He is,' Ashtat says. 'But he must have use for the living dead too. His mutants are clearly not enough for him. He wishes to recruit our kind also.'

'He should be so lucky,' Shane says witheringly. 'If he ever tries to sign me up for *Team Dowling*, I'll shove those spiders where the sun don't shine.'

'I'm sure that will make him quake in his boots,' Carl sneers.

'Do you know anything about Mr Dowling?' I ask before a fight breaks out between the snob and the chav.

'Not much,' Ashtat answers. 'And it is not our place to tell you what we know. Dr Oystein will do that when he returns.'

'You're all in love with that bloody doctor, aren't you?'

'He has given us a home,' Ashtat says. 'He has given our

lives meaning. He has rescued us from an unliving hell and made us feel almost human. Of course we love him. You will too when you realise how fortunate you are to have been taken in by someone as accepting and forgiving as Dr Oystein.'

'I don't need his forgiveness,' I snort.

'No?' Ashtat asks quietly, eyeing me seriously.

I think about Tyler Bayor. Sister Clare of the Shnax. How I wasn't able to save Mark.

I go quiet.

'Grub's up!' someone calls out brightly. Looking up, I spot a smiling lady in a flowery apron entering the room, pushing a trolley loaded with bowls. It's the woman I noticed when Dr Oystein was first showing me around, the one who was scooping brains out of heads.

The Angels around me cheer loudly, as do all the others. The elegantly dressed dinner lady beams and takes a bow, then starts handing out the bowls.

'This is Ciara,' Ashtat says as she approaches our table. 'Ciara, this is Becky Smith, but she likes to be called B.'

'Pleasure to meet you, B,' Ciara says cheerfully. She looks more like a model than any dinner lady I ever met, with high cheekbones, carefully maintained hair, and clothes you'd only find in exclusive boutiques. Even the apron, white cap and green plastic gloves look more suited to a catwalk than a kitchen. But there's one thing about her that's far more extraordinary than her glamorous appearance.

She has a heartbeat.

'You're alive!' I gasp, the beat of her heart like a drum to my sensitive ears.

'Just about,' Ciara grins. 'But don't go thinking that means you can eat my brain. There should be more than enough for you there.'

She hands me a bowl filled with a familiar grey, gloopy substance. It's what the zom heads were fed in the underground complex, human brains mixed up in a semi-appetising way.

'For afters,' Ciara says, slamming a bucket down in the middle of the table. She winks at me. 'Don't be offended if I don't stick around, but I can't stand all the vomiting. Come and have a chat with me later if you want. I used to work in Bow long ago, which – if I'm any judge of an accent – isn't too far from your neck of the woods. I'm sure we'll find plenty to talk about.'

Ciara sticks out a hand and pretends to ruffle my hair, only she doesn't quite touch me. Can't, since she's human and I'm not. I'd probably contaminate her if one of my hairs pierced her glove and stabbed into her flesh. I'm pretty sure that every cell of my body is toxic.

'I didn't expect to find living people here,' I remark as Ciara leaves.

'There aren't many,' Carl says, 'but we get a few passing through, and Ciara is a permanent fixture.'

'She was here when we first moved in,' Ashtat explains. 'She worked in one of the hotel restaurants. Dr Oystein calls her the queen of the dinner ladies. She's so stylish, isn't she? I asked her once why she chose to follow such a career. She said because she liked it, and we should all do what we like in life.'

'Isn't she afraid of being turned into one of us?' I ask.

'That cannot happen,' Ashtat says. 'If she was infected, she would become a revived. But no, she is not afraid. She feels safe around us. She knows we would not deliberately turn her. Of course it could happen accidentally if she fell against one of us and got scratched, but she is happy to take that risk. She says there are no guarantees of safety anywhere in this world now.'

'But if she is ever turned, God help the bugger who does it to her,' Shane growls. 'I don't care if it's an accident — if anyone hurts Ciara, I'll come after them with everything I have.'

'You're my hero,' Carl simpers. 'Now shut up and eat.'

Shane scowls but digs in as ordered.

I tuck into the gruel, not bothering with the spoon which Ciara supplied, just tipping it straight into my mouth from the bowl. I used to think it was disgusting, but having had to scoop brains out of skulls to survive since leaving the under-ground complex, I'm less fussy now.

Jakob is first to finish – he doesn't eat all of his gruel – and he reaches for the bucket and turns aside, sticking a couple of fingers down his throat. The rest of us follow his example when we're ready and the room comes alive with the sound of a few dozen zombies throwing up.

The children of the night — what sweet music we make!

THIRTEEN

Nobody says much for a while after we've finished eating and puking. We all look a bit sheepish. It's not easy doing this in public, even for those who've been living together as Angels for months. It feels like having a dump in front of your friends. I've done a lot of crazy things over the years, but I drew the line at that! Yet here we are, all thirty plus of us, looking like we've been caught with our pants down around our ankles.

Ashtat pulls something out of a pocket, closes her hands over it and starts to pray silently. I roll my eyes at the boys and make a gagging motion, but they don't laugh. When Ashtat finishes and unclasps her hands, I see that the object is a crucifix.

'What are you doing with that?' I ask.

'Praying.'

'With a cross? Don't you guys use ... I don't know ... but not a cross. Those are for us lot.'

'*Us lot?*' Ashtat repeats icily.

'Christians.'

'What makes you think I'm not a Christian?'

I snort. 'You're an Arab. There aren't any Christians in the Middle East.'

'Actually there are,' Ashtat says tightly. 'Quite a few, for your information.'

'I'm not talking about people who go there on pilgrimage,' I sniff.

'Nor am I,' she says. 'I'm talking about Arab Christians.'

'Pull the other one,' I laugh.

Ashtat raises an eyebrow. 'You don't think you can be both an Arab and a Christian?'

'Of course not. You're one or the other.'

'Really?' she jeers. 'So you think that all Arabs are Muslims?'

'Yeah,' I mutter, although I'm getting the sinking feeling that I'm on a hiding to nothing. 'You all worship Allah.'

'And who is Allah?' she presses.

'Your god.'

'No,' she barks. '*Our* god. God and Allah are one and the same. Assuming you believe in God.'

'Well, I'm not religious, but if I did believe, it would be in God, not Allah.'

'As I just told you,' she says, 'Allah *is* God. Our religions have the same roots. Muslims believe in the Old Testament

239

and they revere Christ, Mary and all the saints that Christians do.'

I scratch my head and stare at her, lost for words.

'You don't know anything about Islam, do you?' she says.

'Not really, no,' I admit grudgingly.

Ashtat starts to laugh, then grimaces. 'I'm sorry. I should not mock you for being ignorant. In my experience, most of your people knew nothing about mine. We were just potential terrorists in your eyes.'

I want to protest but I can't, because it's the truth.

'I'm not going to give you a history lesson,' Ashtat goes on. 'If you are truly interested, you can look up the facts yourself. But Muslims and Christians – Jews too – all started out in the same place and believe in the same God. We branched along the way, but at our core we are the same.

'I'm Muslim,' she continues, 'but one of my grandmothers was Christian. She converted when she came to this country and married my grandfather, but she told her children and grandchildren about her old beliefs and encouraged us to respect Christianity. The Virgin Mary was her favourite and I often say a prayer to her, thinking of my grandmother, especially in these troubled times.'

Ashtat stops and waits for me to respond. I can only gawp at her. It's like I've been told that the Earth actually is flat or the moon truly is made of cheese.

'Why did your people hate us if that's the case?' Shane asks. This is obviously news to him too.

'Why did *your* people hate *us*?' Ashtat retorts.

'Because of September the tenth and all the other crap,' Shane says.

'You mean September the eleventh,' Carl sighs, rolling his eyes.

'What about the Crusades?' Ashtat counters. 'Western Christians tried to wipe out my people, to steal our land and treasures. Later, in the twentieth century, you divided up our nations as it suited you, to govern us as you saw fit. You . . .' She shakes her head. 'We could argue about this forever, but it would not do any good. I don't hate anyone or blame anyone or see myself as being part of any army except the army of the Angels. The old grudges seem ridiculous now that the world has changed so much.'

'You're the one who started the argument,' I pout.

'I was not arguing,' she contradicts me. 'I was simply pointing out a matter of fact, in response to your assertion that Arabs could not also be Christians.'

'All right. I stand corrected. Happy now?'

'Yes,' Ashtat says, putting away her crucifix.

'I didn't mean any harm,' I add softly.

She smiles. 'I know. Forget about it.'

'My dad . . .' I consider telling them how I was raised, about my racist father, what happened with Tyler, how I'm

241

trying to be different. But before I can decide how to start, a Chinese guy enters the dining room and claps loudly.

All conversation comes to an immediate halt. Everyone rises and bows. The newcomer waits a moment, then bows smoothly in return. When he straightens, he looks around, spots me and comes across.

He's a bit taller than me, although not a lot older, maybe five or six years my senior, dressed in jeans and a white T-shirt. No shoes. Bones jut out of his toes and fingers. They've been carefully trimmed into dagger-like tips.

He stops in front of me. I'm the only person still sitting. I glance at the others but they don't look at me. Their gazes are fixed dead ahead.

'I am Master Zhang,' he says softly. 'In future you will stand and bow when you see me.'

'Why?' I snap.

His right hand flickers and before I can react, his fingers are tightening round my throat. I slap at his arm and try to pull free, but he holds firm.

'Because I will kill you if you do not,' he says without changing tone.

'Don't ... need ... breath,' I growl. 'You ... can't ... choke ... me.'

'No. But I can rip your head from your neck and dig into your brain. I could do it now. I would not even need to alter my grip. Do you doubt that?'

I stare into his dark brown eyes – one of them is badly bloodshot – and shake my head stiffly.

'Good,' he says, releasing me. 'That is a start. Now you will stand, bow and say my name.'

I want to tell him to get stuffed, but I've a feeling my head would be sent rolling across the floor before I got to the end of the insult. I don't think this guy plays games, that he's someone you can push to a certain point. You show him respect or he rips your apart, simple as that.

Pushing my chair back, I stand, bow and mutter as politely as I can, 'Master Zhang.'

'Good,' he says again, then turns to face Carl. 'You will bring her to me when you are finished here. I will test her.'

'Yes, Master Zhang,' Carl says, bowing again.

Zhang leaves without saying anything else. Once he's gone, the Angels sit and conversation resumes as if we were never interrupted.

I rub my throat and glare at the others. 'You could have warned me,' I snarl.

Carl waves away my accusation. 'We all have to go through that. Master Zhang likes to make his own introductions.'

'Do you really think he would have ripped my head off?' I ask.

'If you were dumb enough to assume he was joking, yes,' Carl says. 'But so far nobody's made that mistake. Even

Shane knew better than to give Master Zhang any grief.'

'I'd like to see him tear someone's head off though,' Shane says. He shoots me a quick look. 'I was hoping *you* might talk back to him, just to see what he'd do.'

'Good to know you have my back if things ever get ugly,' I snarl. For a few seconds I consider walking out the door and leaving — in some ways this place is just as bad as the underground complex where I was held prisoner. But where would I go? Who could I turn to? Grumbling darkly, I sit down like the rest of them. 'So that guy's your mentor?' I ask, recalling what Awnya said when she mentioned him.

'Yes,' Ashtat says. 'He teaches us how to fight and fend for ourselves, so that we are ready for the missions on which we are sent.'

'Just him?'

'Yes. He is the only tutor we need.'

'And the test he mentioned?'

Ashtat snickers. 'Every Angel trains with Master Zhang, but some are deemed more worthy of his attention than others. He will take your measure when you spar with him. If he is impressed, you will train to join the likes of us on life-or-death missions.'

'If you disappoint him,' Carl says, 'you'll end up rooting through shops for supplies with the twins.'

'Or mixing up brains with Ciara to put in the gruel,' Shane giggles.

'It's time to find out if you're a lion or a lamb,' Ashtat says.

'I'm no bloody lamb,' I growl.

She purses her lips. 'No, I do not think that you are.' Then her expression softens and she adds hauntingly, 'Although if you are cleared to come on missions with us, you might end up wishing that you were.'

FOURTEEN

When everyone's had their fill, they stack up the bowls and leave them on the tables, then file out of the dining room. Carl tells me to accompany him to the gym for my test with Master Zhang. I expect the others to come with us, but they head off to do their own thing.

'This won't be the gladiatorial showdown of the year,' Carl smirks, noting my disappointment.

'What do you mean?'

'It's not going to be some amazing duel, with you pushing Master Zhang all the way. The test for newbies is pretty boring. That's why no one's interested.'

'Maybe I'll surprise you,' I grunt.

'No,' he says. 'You won't.'

Carl takes me by the swimming pool on our way. A couple of Angels are doing laps, moving faster than any Olympic swimmer, like a pair of sharks following a trail of blood.

'Can you swim?' Carl asks.

'Yeah.'

'You're free to train here whenever you want,' he says. 'But make sure you plug up your nostrils and ears — water will lodge if you don't. And keep your mouth firmly shut. Liquids slip down our throats easily enough, but they're a real pain to get rid of. Trust me, unless you like wearing nappies, you don't want to go sloshing around with a few litres of water inside you.'

'I'll bear that in mind.'

The gym is fairly standard, cross-trainers, rowing machines, weights and so on. Several Angels are working out, some under the gaze of Master Zhang, others by themselves.

Master Zhang ignores me for a few minutes, studying a girl as she performs a series of gymnastic routines in front of a dummy that must have been brought here from a shop. Each spin or twirl ends with a flick of a hand or foot to the dummy's head or torso. She's already chipped away at a lot of it, and keeps on tearing in, cracking it, knocking chunks loose, ignoring the cuts and nicks she's picking up.

'Keep going until there is nothing left to destroy,' Master Zhang says to the girl, then strides for the door, nodding at Carl and me to follow.

He leads us to a bare room that looks like it was once a conference room for high-flying businessmen. Any chairs and tables have been removed, though there are still some whiteboards on the walls.

'Each revitalised is different,' Master Zhang says, wasting no time on chit-chat. 'Our bodies react uniquely when we return to life. There are similarities common to all – extra strength and speed – but nobody can judge the extent of their abilities until they test themself. Physical build is not a factor. Some of us have great potential. Others do not.

'We can fine-tune whatever skills we possess, but if you are found lacking at this stage, you will forever be limited by the restraints of your body. When you died, you lost the capacity to improve on what nature provided you with. In short, your response to today's test will decide your role within the Angels for the next few thousand years. So I suggest you apply yourself as best you can.'

Master Zhang marches me to one end of the room, then tells me to make a standing jump. I crouch, tense the muscles in my legs, then spring forward like a frog. I hurtle almost two-thirds of the way across the room, far further than any human could have ever jumped. I'm delighted with myself, but when I look at Master Zhang, he makes a so-so gesture.

'Carl,' he says and Carl copies what I did, only he sails past me and bounces off the wall ahead of us.

'Does that mean I've failed?' I ask bitterly.

'No,' Master Zhang said. 'It simply means that if someone

is required to leap across a great distance – for instance, from the roof of one building to another – we will choose Carl or another like him.'

Next we step out into the corridor and I perform a running jump. I do better this time, although still nowhere near what Carl can do. Then Master Zhang times me racing up and down. He's pleased with my speed. 'Not the fastest by any means, but quicker than many.'

We step back into the room and Master Zhang tests my sense of balance by having me stand in a variety of uncomfortable positions and hold the pose as long as I can. Then he tests my reflexes by lobbing small, hard balls at me. Again he's happy with my response, but far from overwhelmed.

We return to the gym and he tries me out with weights. I come up short on this one. Others are lifting weights around me and I can see that I don't match up. I lift far more than I could have when I was alive, but ultimately I fall low down the pecking order.

'Do not look so upset,' Master Zhang says as I step away from the weights, feeling defeated. 'I am by no means the strongest person here, but that has never worked against me. I taught myself how to deal with stronger opponents many years ago and my foes have yet to get the better of me.'

'Have a lot of foes, do you?' I laugh.

'Yes,' he says simply, not bothering to elaborate.

Then it's back to the conference room, where Master

Zhang has me face him. Carl watches from a spot near the door, grinning eagerly.

'This is the part you have probably been looking forward to,' Master Zhang says. 'I am going to test your sharpness and wit. I want you to try to hit me, first with your fists, then with your feet. You can use any move you wish, a punch, chop, slap, whatever.'

'Shouldn't we be in karate or boxing gear for this sort of thing?' I ask.

'No. We do not wear special clothes when we fight in the world outside, so why should we wear them here? I want to see how you will perform on the streets, where it matters.'

With a shrug, I eye up Master Zhang, then jab a fist at his nose. He shimmies and my fist whistles through thin air. I expected as much, and also guessed the way he would move, so even while he's ducking, I'm bringing up my other fist to hit him from the opposite side.

Master Zhang grabs my arm and stops my fist short of its target.

'Good,' he says, releasing me. 'Again.'

I spend the next ten minutes trying to strike him with my fists, then ten trying to hit him with my feet. I fare better with my feet than fists, connecting with his shoulders and midriff a number of times, and once – sweetly – with the side of his face. I don't cause any damage but I can tell he's impressed.

'Rest a while,' he says, taking a step back.

'I didn't think zombies needed rest.'

'Even the living dead need rest,' he says. 'We are more enduring than we were in life, but our bodies do have limits. If we demand too much of ourselves, it affects our performance. We can struggle on indefinitely, sluggishly, but our battles need to be fought on our terms. It is not enough to be dogged. We must be incisive.'

'Who do we fight?' I ask. 'Mr Dowling and his mutants? Reviveds? The army?'

'Dr Oystein will answer your questions,' Master Zhang says. 'I am here merely to determine how useful you might be to us and to help you make the most of your talents.'

Master Zhang spends the next ten minutes throwing punches and kicks at me. I manage to duck or block many of them, but plenty penetrate and by the end of the session I'm stinging all over. But it's a good kind of pain and I don't mind.

After opening up a small cut beneath my right eye, Master Zhang says, 'That will be enough. Return tomorrow. I want to see how your cuts moss over.'

'What do you mean?' I ask.

'We cannot heal as we could when we were alive,' he explains. 'Moss grows in places where we are cut, but it sprouts more thickly in some than in others. If the moss grows thinly over your cuts, you will continue to lose blood when you fight, which will affect your performance, making you of little use to us.'

'Nothing wrong with my moss,' I say confidently. 'Look, it's already stitching the wound closed, I can feel it.' I tilt my head backwards, so that he can see.

Master Zhang smiles thinly. 'I believe that it is. But as I said, come back to see me tomorrow, and we will test it then.'

'Assuming the moss grows thickly,' I call after him as he turns to leave, 'how did I do on the rest of the tests? Am I good enough to be a proper Angel with Carl and the others?'

Master Zhang pauses and casts a slow look over me with his bloodshot left eye. I feel like I'm being X-rayed.

'Physically, yes, my feeling is that you are, although there are a few more tests that you must complete before we can say for certain. Mentally?' He looks unsure. 'Most living people fear death more than anything else, but our kind need not, since we have already died. So tell me, Becky Smith, what do you fear more than anything else now?'

I think about telling him that I don't fear anything, but that wouldn't be the truth. And I think about saying that I fear Mr Dowling, Owl Man and the mutants, but while I'm certainly scared of the killer clown and his strange associates, they're not the ones who gnaw away at my nerves deep down. I'm sure that if I'm not totally honest with Master Zhang, he'll pick up on the deception and it will go against me. So, even though I hate having to admit it, I tell him.

'I'm afraid of myself,' I croak, lowering my gaze to hide

my shame. 'I've done some bad things in the past, and I'm afraid, if I don't keep a close watch on myself every single day, that I might do even worse.'

There's a long silence. Then Master Zhang makes a small clucking sound. 'I think you will fit in here,' he says.

And that marks the end of the first round of tests.

FIFTEEN

'I told you it wouldn't be exciting,' Carl says as we head back to our room.

I grunt.

'You'll have to get used to the boredom,' he continues. 'We spend most of our time training. It sounds like it will be great, learning how to fight, and there *are* times when I learn a new move and it feels amazing. But for the most part it's pretty dull.'

There's no one in our room when we get there. Carl changes his shirt – there wasn't anything wrong with the old one, he just wants to try something new – and we head to the front of the building, out on to a large terrace overlooking the river. Carl doesn't stop to admire the view, but hurries down the stairs and along the path.

'Are we going to the London Dungeon?' I ask, spotting a sign for it.

Carl gives me an odd look. 'Isn't the world grisly enough for you as it is?'

'But the Dungeon's fun,' I laugh.

'It used to be,' he agrees. 'Not so much now that there aren't any actors to bring the place to life. We sometimes train down there, but we don't really make use of it otherwise. It's not a fun place to hang out.'

'Do the rides still work?' I ask.

'Yes,' he says.

'Come on. Let's try them.'

'Maybe later,' he says, then heads for the old arcade centre. I could go and explore the Dungeon by myself, but I don't want to be alone so, with a scowl, I follow him.

Most of the video games in the arcade still seem to be operational, but although a handful of Angels are hanging around, nobody's playing. That seems strange to me until I recall my advanced sense of hearing and the way bright lights hurt my eyes. I guess half an hour on a video game in my current state would be about as much fun as sticking my hand into a food blender.

Our lot are bowling. They have the lanes to themselves. Jakob is taking his turn as we approach. He knocks down the four standing pins and gets a spare.

'Nice one,' Shane says.

Jakob only shrugs. I've never seen anyone who looks as

miserable as this guy. I wonder what it would take to make him smile.

'How did the test go?' Ashtat asks as we slip in beside her.

'I aced it. Master Zhang said I was the best student he'd ever seen.'

'Sure,' she drawls. 'I bet he got down on his knees and worshipped you.'

We grin at each other. We got off on the wrong foot, but I'm starting to warm to the Muslim girl, which is something I never thought I'd hear myself admit.

Shane hits the gutter and swears.

'You're lucky Master Zhang wasn't here to see that,' Carl tuts.

'Why?' I ask. 'Don't tell me he's a master bowler too.'

'It's part of our training,' Shane sighs, waiting for his ball to return. 'He says bowling is good for concentration. Our eyes aren't as sharp as they were, and no amount of drops will ever change that. We have to keep working on our hand to eye coordination.'

'Eye to hand,' Carl corrects him.

'Whatever,' Shane mutters and throws again. This time he knocks down seven pins but he's not happy. He flexes his fingers and glares at them as if they're to blame.

Ashtat throws and gets a strike. Jakob steps up next, then pauses and offers me the ball.

'Don't you want to finish the game?' I ask.

'No,' he whispers. 'It doesn't matter.'

I take the ball from him and test the holes. They're too small for my fingers – I cast a quick glance at Jakob and note how unnaturally thin he is – so I put it back and find one that fits. I take aim, step up and let the ball rip.

It shoots down the lane faster than I would have thought possible and smashes into the pins, sending them scattering in every direction. A few of them shatter and go flying across the adjacent lanes.

'Bloody hell!' I gasp, shocked and dismayed. 'I'm sorry. I didn't mean to ...'

I stop. The others are laughing. Even Jakob is smiling slightly. Shane high-fives the thin, bald kid, then slaps my back. 'Don't worry. That happens to most of us the first time.'

'We're stronger than we look,' Ashtat says. 'We have to learn to control our strength. That's another of the reasons we practise here.'

'You could have told me that before I threw,' I say sourly.

'It wouldn't have been as funny then,' Carl giggles.

'No,' I smile. 'I guess it wouldn't.'

We move to another lane while Jakob clears up the mess and replaces the pins. It takes me a while to get the balance right – I throw the first few balls too softly, then hit the gutters when I lob more forcefully – but eventually I find my groove. It's tricky to be accurate because of my weak eyesight, but I can compensate for that by throwing a bit harder than I did when alive.

After a couple of games – I finish last the first time, but fourth in the next game, ahead of a disgusted Shane – we spill out of the arcade. Night has fallen and dark clouds drift across the sky. I suggest the Dungeon again, but the others say they want to go on the London Eye. I'm curious to see what the city looks like now from up high, so I don't argue.

We step into one of the pods and rise. I turn slowly as we ascend, taking in the three hundred and sixty degree view. As I'm turning, I spot an Angel sitting on the bench in the middle of a pod on the opposite side of the big wheel, staring solemnly out over the river.

'What's up with that guy?' I ask.

'He's a lookout,' Carl says. 'There's always an Angel on duty in the Eye, in touch with a guard inside County Hall, in case we get attacked by Mr Dowling and his mutant army. They use walkie-talkies — mobile phones don't work any more.'

'I noticed that,' I frown. 'Any idea why not?'

'It's the end of the world,' Carl says. 'Lots of things don't work.'

'I know, but I thought mobiles would be all right, since they operate through satellites.'

'You thought wrong,' Carl sniffs. 'That's why we rely on

the walkie-talkies. You'll be posted to a pod once you settle in. We all have to take our turn, even the twins and those who don't come on missions.'

'Except for One-eyed Pete,' Ashtat says.

'Obviously,' Carl replies.

I whistle, impressed. 'There's really an Angel called One-eyed Pete?'

Carl and Ashtat gaze at me serenely and I realise I've taken the bait, hook, line and sinker.

'All right,' I growl as they burst out laughing. 'I'm an idiot. I admit it. Just throw me off this thing when we get to the top and have done with me.'

We chat away as the pod glides upwards, admiring the view over County Hall, looking down on the roof and into the courtyards. I try to spot the room where the Groove Tubes are, but it's hard to be sure.

'I came up here a few times with my mum and dad when I was younger,' I mumble, remembering happier days when the world wasn't a nightmarish place.

'What happened to them?' Ashtat asks quietly.

'I don't know. I think Dad might have made it out. Mum ...' I shake my head, wondering again about her, hoping she's alive, but not able to believe that she is. And Dad? Well, it's kind of the opposite with him. I'm pretty sure he slipped away, but part of me hopes he didn't, that he paid for what he made me do to Tyler. But I don't *want* to feel that way. He's my dad, and as much as I hate him for what he is – what he always was – I love him too.

'How about the rest of you?' I ask. 'Did you all lose family?'

'Yes,' Ashtat says. 'Parents, brothers, sisters ...'

'A girlfriend,' Shane adds morosely.

'A boyfriend,' Carl sighs, then winks at a startled Shane. 'Only joking.'

'You'd better be,' Shane huffs. 'I'm not sharing a room with you if not.'

Carl fakes a gasp. 'Hark at the homophobe! Just for that, I'm going to convert. Come here, you big sap, and give me a kiss.'

They wrestle and stumble around the pod, Carl laughing, Shane cursing. The rest of us look on wearily.

'Boys never change, do they?' I note.

'Sadly, no,' Ashtat murmurs. 'They might have lost their carnal appetites, but that won't stop them being bothersome little pests.'

'Lost their ...? Oh yeah, I forgot about that.'

Apparently zombies can't get down and dirty — none of the necessary equipment is in working order. Apart from snogging – which probably isn't much fun with a dry tongue and cold lips – there's not much we can do.

Shane and Carl break apart. Both are grinning. Then Carl's expression darkens as he recalls what we were talking about.

'I went to the offices where my father used to work once I'd revitalised. I found him there. He's a revived now. I thought about killing him but I didn't dare, just in case anyone ever discovered a cure for them.'

'You know that won't happen,' Ashtat says sympathetically.

'Yeah, but still . . .'

'Your dad might revitalise,' I say, trying to cheer him up.

Carl squints at me. 'What are you talking about?'

'Well, we recovered our senses, so maybe he will too.'

'He can't,' Carl says. 'He wasn't vaccinated.'

'What?' I frown.

'Leave it.' Ashtat stops Carl before he can continue. 'Dr Oystein will explain it when he returns.'

'I'm getting sick of hearing that,' I growl. 'What is he, the bloody keeper of all secrets? Are you afraid the world will go up in flames if you tell me something behind his back?'

'It's just simpler if he tells you,' Ashtat says calmly. 'He's used to explaining. If we tried, we might confuse you.'

'At least you admit that you don't know what the hell you're talking about,' I mutter, then cast an eye over Jakob who, as usual, is standing silently by the rest of us. 'What about you, skeleton boy? Did zombies eat your nearest and dearest, or did they leave Ma and Pa Addams alone?'

Jakob stares at me uncertainly, then gets the reference. 'Oh. I see. I look like one of the Addams Family. Very funny.'

'You bitch,' Ashtat snarls.

'What?' I snap. 'Aren't we allowed to have a go at skin-heads any more?'

'You don't think he shaved himself, do you?' she asks.

'Well, yeah, of course. I mean why else ...?'

I stop and wince. How dumb am I? Pale skin. Bald. Dark circles under his eyes. Skinny in an unhealthy way.

'You've got cancer, haven't you?' I groan.

'Yes,' Jakob says softly. 'It was terminal. I was close to the end. I had maybe a few weeks left to live. Then I was bitten. Now I'm going to be like this forever.'

'Is the cancer still active?' I ask. 'Will it carry on eating you up?'

'No,' he sighs. 'But it hasn't gone away. It still hurts. I can ignore the pain and function normally when I focus, which is why I'm allowed to go on missions, but the rest of the time I feel weak, tired and disoriented. It's why I often seem spaced out.'

'I'm sorry. Really. I wouldn't have had a go at you if I'd known.'

He waves away my apology. 'It doesn't matter. Nothing that you said could hurt me. Nobody could. Not after ...'

He stops and I think he's going to clam up again. But then he continues, his voice the barest of whispers, so that even with my sharp ears I have to strain to catch every word.

'I'd come to London with my parents and younger sister.

One last visit. Nobody phrased it that way but we all knew. Our final day out together. Mum and Dad took time off work, even though they couldn't afford to — they were struggling to make ends meet, having spent so much on me over the last few years.

'We got delayed on our way down, so we had to cut out some of the things we'd planned to do. In the end we went to Trafalgar Square first. I loved the lions, the fountains, looking up at the National Gallery.'

I consider telling him what happened the last time I was in Trafalgar Square, but I don't dare interrupt him in case he goes silent again.

'We had lunch in the crypt in St Martin-in-the-Fields. I had a Scotch egg. I knew it would make me sick – my stomach couldn't handle rich food – but I didn't care. It was sort of my last supper. I wanted it to be special.' He smiles fleetingly. 'That's how bad things get when you're that close to death. A Scotch egg becomes something special.'

Jakob retreats from the window and sits on the bench. Rests his hands on his knees and carries on talking. No one else makes a sound. If we could hold our breath – if we had breath to hold – we would.

'I was one of the first to be attacked when zombies spilled into the crypt. In a way that was a mercy. I didn't have to witness the madness and terror which must have surely followed.

'I was still in the crypt when I regained my senses weeks later. I'd made a base there, along with dozens of others. I'd fashioned a cot out of a few of the corpses. I suppose it was a bed cum larder, as I'd eaten from them too. I know that because I was eating when I revitalised, digging my fingers into a skull, scraping out a few dry, tasteless scraps of brain.

'It was my sister's skull,' he says, and the most horrible thing about it is that his tone doesn't change. It's like he's telling us the time. 'My mum and dad were there too. Well, in my dad's case it was just his head. I couldn't find his body. I did search for it but . . .'

Jakob pauses, then decides to stop. He lowers his head and starts to massage his neck. Nobody says anything.

Without discussing it, we spread out around the pod, giving Jakob some privacy. We stare at the river and the buildings, smoke rising into the air from a number of places, corpses strewn everywhere, abandoned boats and cars, paths and roads stained with blood, black in the dim night light.

I think about asking Ashtat if I can borrow her cross. But I don't. And it's not because I don't want to be a hypocrite and say a prayer to a God I barely believe in. It's because I figure what's the point in saying any prayers for this broken, bloodied city of the ungodly dead?

SIXTEEN

Carl wasn't joking about training being boring. Over the next three days I perform the same routines over and over — swim (having carefully plugged up my nose and ears), work out in the gym and get thrown around the hollow conference room by the stone-faced Master Zhang.

'It is important that you learn how to fall correctly,' he says when I complain after being slammed down hard on the floorboards for the hundredth time. 'In a fight, you will often be thrown or knocked over. If you can cushion your landing, you will be in a better position to carry on.'

'How long will I have to do this?' I grumble, rubbing my bruised shoulders. I'm beginning to wish he'd ruled me unfit for active service.

'Until I am satisfied,' he says and hurls me over his shoulder again.

I'm keen to learn all sorts of cool moves, and disgusted by

what I consider a waste of my time, so I leave the sessions with a face like thunder, but Ashtat tells me I have to be patient. They all had to endure this to begin with.

'Master Zhang wants to turn you into a fighting machine,' she explains. 'That isn't a simple task. You should be thankful he's spending so much time on you, even if it is only to throw you around. If he didn't consider you worthy, he would not be proceeding so diligently with you.'

I know she's right, but it's hard to maintain my interest and temper. I was never the most patient of girls. Maybe that's why I didn't have a boyfriend — I couldn't be bothered putting in all the time and effort required.

If I'd come to Master Zhang when I was human, I doubt I'd have stuck with him more than a day. I definitely wouldn't have made it past the second. But things are different now. It's not like I have more attractive options. If I don't play ball here, I can go off by myself, regress and become a shambling revived, or maybe hook up with Mr Dowling and his merry band of mutants. Hardly the sort of career prospects that young girls around the world dream about.

At least I get on pretty well with my room-mates. They're not the sort I would have been friends with in my previous life, but they're not a bad bunch. They do their best to help me find my feet, show me round County Hall, give me tips like how to groom the bones sticking out of my fingers and toes.

I haven't spoken to many of the other Angels. I've picked up names here and there, and I know a few to nod to in the gym and pool – such as Ingrid and her crew – but I haven't tried to bond with any of them. I'm still not sure if this place is for me, and won't know for certain until I've had a chance to chat with Dr Oystein again. If I don't like what I hear, and decide that I'm better off out of it, I don't want the added aggro of having to leave friends behind.

On the afternoon of the fourth day, after lunch, when I have free time on my hands, I head down to the lab with the Groove Tubes to catch up with Reilly, something I've been meaning to do since our first reunion.

The soldier isn't in the lab, nor is Rage, who must have been fished out not long after I was. I get an angry feeling in my gut when I spot the empty Tube, recalling the way Rage threw the rest of the zom heads to the lions, how he killed Dr Cerveris. I'm uneasy too — I don't trust Rage. It wouldn't surprise me if he popped up behind me and dug a knife into the back of my skull.

I ask around and track down Reilly to the kitchen where Ciara works. Reilly and the dinner lady are talking while she washes up. As far as I'm aware, they're the only two humans here, so I guess they feel closer to one another than to the cannibalistic zombies they serve.

'Hey,' Reilly says when he spots me. 'I was wondering when you'd come looking for me.'

'What made you think I would?' I snort.

'I've always known you had a crush on me,' he grins.

'Not if you were the last guy in the world,' I jeer, hopping up on to a table across from the pair and letting my legs dangle. 'Isn't there a dishwasher for that?' I ask Ciara as she scrubs another plate.

'I prefer washing by hand,' she says cheerfully. 'It passes the time and it keeps my mind off . . . other matters.'

Her shoulders shudder slightly and I don't ask any more questions. I'm sure, like any other survivor in this post-apocalyptic city, that she has memories she'd rather not dwell on.

'Go on then,' I say to Reilly. 'Tell me how you came to be here.'

He shrugs. 'There's no big story. Josh and the others who hadn't been killed by the clown and his mutants pulled out of the underground complex in the wake of the assault. I'd had doubts about the place from the beginning. What I saw that day – the way the reviveds and revitaliseds were executed like rabid animals – helped make up my mind. I wanted out, so I walked away while they were evacuating. I doubt if anyone missed me. If they did, they probably assumed I was killed or converted by a stray zombie.'

'Took you long enough to see them for what they were,' I sniff.

Reilly sighs. 'Things aren't black and white any more. They never were, I suppose, but there used to be law and order, right and wrong. Now it's all chaos. I don't think Josh or Dr Cerveris were bad guys. They were trying to uncover answers, to figure out a way to put the world back on track. I didn't approve of how they went about it, but if they'd cracked the zombie gene and come up with a way to rid the world of the living dead . . .'

'They'd have been your heroes?' I sneer.

'Yeah,' he says. 'You've got to remember, *you're* the enemy. Dr Oystein is doing an incredible job, and I admire how his Angels have dedicated themselves to helping the living. But you're all part of the problem. Dr Oystein acknowledges that, so it's not like I'm being disrespectful. The world has been torn apart by a war between the living and the dead, and even though you guys are on my side, I can't trust you. One scrape of those bones, if I stumbled and you instinctively reached out to grab me, and I'm history.'

I frown. 'So why swap Josh for Dr Oystein?'

'I think he can do more than Josh could,' Reilly says. 'He knows more about what makes you lot tick. He's working from within to solve the problem and that gives him an edge over everybody else. I also like the fact that he goes about his business humanely, but I won't kid you, that's just a bonus. If I believed that we could sort out this mess by slicing you up in agonising, brutal ways, you wouldn't get any sympathy from me. I'd feel bad about it, but that wouldn't stop me forging ahead.'

'He says such nasty things sometimes, doesn't he?' Ciara tuts.

'He's no saint, that's for sure,' I mutter.

'Then again, this is hardly a time for saints, is it?' Reilly notes.

'True,' I nod. 'So how'd you find your way here? Did you follow the arrows?'

'No.' Reilly scratches the back of his neck. 'I was on my way out of the city. I wanted to join a compound in the countryside or head for one of the zombie-free islands and try to gain entry. Then I ran into a pack of Angels on a mission. I would have avoided them, except I recognised someone with them. I tracked the pack until he parted company with the zombies, then revealed myself and asked what he was up to. When he explained what was going on here, I decided I wanted to be part of it. I offered my services. They were accepted. So here I am.'

'Who was the guy you recognised?' I ask.

'You'll find out soon,' Reilly says. 'Dr Oystein returned earlier today and my contact was with him. I'm guessing the pair of them will want to see you.'

I get a prickle of excitement when I hear that the mysterious doctor is back. I was starting to think that I'd only dreamt about him. It seems like months since he introduced himself to me and took me on my first tour of the building.

'One last question. Do you know where Rage is?'

Reilly grimaces. 'We hauled him out of the Tube a couple of days ago. I've been watching my back since then.'

I bare my teeth in a vicious grin. 'I thought you trusted him.'

'I never said that,' Reilly corrects me. 'I said that Dr Oystein trusts him, and I trust Dr Oystein. I protected Rage because the doctor asked me to. That doesn't mean I liked it. And it doesn't mean I feel safe now that he's out on the prowl.'

Reilly looks around nervously and touches the handle of the stun gun which he has strapped to his side. 'Truth be told, I'm crapping myself.'

I laugh harshly. 'You should become one of us, Reilly. We don't crap, we just vomit.'

With that, I hop down and head back to the gym, treading carefully, judging the shadows as I pass, on the lookout for a cherubic monster.

SEVENTEEN

Now that Dr Oystein is back, I expect him to summon me for a meeting, but there's no sign of him that evening or night, and I head to bed at the usual time, surprised and frustrated.

When I mention the doctor's return to the others, they're not that bothered. Shane and Jakob say that they already knew. Ashtat and Carl didn't, but it's not a big deal for them, since they're accustomed to him coming and going.

'I never thought to tell you,' Shane shrugs when I ask why he didn't let me know. 'It's not like we announce it with bugles every time he returns.'

In the morning I report for training again with Master Zhang. He lobs me around and slams me down hard on my back, time after time, studying the way I land, making suggestions, urging me to twist an arm this way, a leg that way.

After one particularly vicious slam dunk that makes me

cry out loud, someone gasps theatrically and says, 'I hope that's as painful as it looks from here.'

I glance around, spirits rising, thinking it must be Dr Oystein, even though that would be a strange thing for him to say. But it's not the doctor. It's Rage, standing by the wall and smirking.

'Nice to see you again, Becky,' Rage says with fake sweetness. 'Last time I saw you, you were hanging naked in the Groove Tube.'

'Same here,' I sneer. 'Sorry for your little problem.'

'What do you mean?'

I cock the smallest finger on my right hand and flex it a couple of times.

Rage laughs. 'I don't worry about those sorts of things any more. You'll have to do better than that to wind me up.'

'I'll do my best,' I snarl.

'Do you get the feeling she doesn't like me?' Rage asks Master Zhang.

'I have no interest in your petty squabbles,' Zhang says as I stand and grimace, still aching from when he threw me. 'In my company, you will treat one another with respect, as all of my students must.'

'You've been training Rage too?' I ask.

'For the last couple of days, yes,' Zhang nods.

'Be careful what you teach him,' I growl. 'He might use it against you.'

'Now, now, Becky,' Rage smiles. 'Remember what Master Zhang told you. It's all about *respect*.'

'Respect this,' I spit, giving him the finger.

'Enough,' Zhang says quietly. 'I will not tolerate disobedience.'

'Hear that?' Rage beams. 'You're gonna have a hard time –'

'That applies to you as well,' Zhang stops him. 'Both of you will be silent.'

I expect Rage to challenge Master Zhang, but he shuts up immediately and bows politely. I glare at him but hold my tongue.

'Oystein told me of your feud,' Zhang says, 'but that is not why I have kept you apart. I prefer to train new recruits by themselves for the first few days, so that I can evaluate them independently.'

'I bet I'm doing better than you,' Rage murmurs to me.

I ignore him, as does Master Zhang.

'There is a test that I subject my students to, usually after a couple of weeks,' Zhang continues. 'But Oystein wishes to speak with both of you later today, to explain more about our history and goals. I have decided to give you the test ahead of that meeting.'

'Why?' Rage asks.

'It is an important test,' Zhang says. 'If you fail, it will be an indication that you are not cut out for life as a fully active

Angel. If Oystein knows that you will not be taking part in our more serious missions, it might affect what he chooses to share with you.'

'You mean, if we turn out to be a pair of losers, he won't want to waste too much time on us,' I grunt.

'Precisely,' Zhang says smoothly, then heads to the door and nods for us to follow him.

'You're not giving us the test here?' Rage asks as we turn into the corridor.

'No,' he says. 'We need reviveds for the test.' He looks back at us and his eyes glitter. '*Lots* of reviveds.'

Rage and I share a worried glance, then trail Master Zhang through the building. He stops off at a small storage room to pick up a couple of rucksacks, then leads us outside and over to Waterloo Station. We pass one of the speakers along the way, but he doesn't bother to turn it off.

'What's that noise?' Rage winces.

'I'll tell you about it sometime, if you pass this test,' I grin, delighted to know something he doesn't.

Zhang leads us up to the station concourse. This used to be one of the busiest train stations in London, but now it's home to hundreds of resting reviveds. The mindless zombies are scattered around the concourse, squatting, sitting, lying down, or just standing, waiting for night to fall. It's strange to think that so many of them are on our doorstep. I haven't seen any since I came to County Hall.

I stare at the old ticket machines, the shops and restaurants, trying to recall what it would have been like back in the day, wanting to feel nostalgic. But it's getting harder to remember what the world was like, to treat the memories as if they're real, rather than fragments of some crazy dream I once had.

'This is a very straightforward task,' Zhang says. He points towards the far end of the concourse, to an open doorway at the rear of the station. 'I want you to race to that exit. If you make it out in one piece, you pass the test.'

'That's all?' Rage frowns. 'But that's too easy. The zombies won't attack us. They know we're the same as them. Unless these are different to the ones I've seen elsewhere?'

'They are no different,' Zhang says. 'I did not arrange for them to be present, or interfere with them in any way. These are the usual residents, reviveds who have chosen to base themselves here.'

'Then what's the catch?' Rage asks.

'The rucksacks of course,' I tell him.

'Correct,' Zhang says. He passes one of the rucksacks to me, the other to Rage, and gestures at us to put them on.

'I still don't get it,' Rage growls. 'They're not heavy. They won't slow us down.'

'They are not meant to slow you down,' Master Zhang tuts, then drives the fingers of his right hand into the rucksack on Rage's back, making five holes in it, before doing the same thing to mine.

The scent of fresh brains instantly fills the air and my lips tighten.

'This isn't good,' Rage mutters as the heads of the zombies closest to us start to lift.

'If you stood still, they would come and examine you,' Zhang says. 'When they realised that the brains are stored in your rucksacks, they'd let you be – reviveds do not fight with one another – and stand nearby, waiting, hoping to finish off any scraps that you might leave behind.'

'But we're not going to stand still, are we?' I sigh.

'No,' Zhang says. 'You are going to run.' He pokes some more holes in our rucksacks. '*Now.*'

Rage swears under his breath and shoots a dirty look at Master Zhang. Then, since he has no other choice, he runs towards the zombies, who are stirring and getting to their feet. And since I have no choice either, I race after him, closing in quickly on the growing, undead wall of snarling, hungry reviveds.

EIGHTEEN

Rage barrels into several of the zombies, sending them flying. They howl with anger and excitement, more of them becoming alert, catching the scent of brains, closing in on us, fangs bared, finger bones twitching.

I take advantage of the confusion Rage has caused and angle to the right, hoping to slip by unnoticed. But other zombies who were sheltering on the platforms have heard the noises and come to investigate. When they spot me tearing by, they clamber over the ticket barriers and surge towards me in a mob, forcing me back into the centre of the concourse.

Rage is surrounded and is lashing out with his fists, trying to shove past those who block his way. It looks impossible, but he's kept up his momentum, like a burly rugby player forcing back a scrum.

I take a different approach. As zombies clutch at me and

278

throw themselves in my path, I duck and shimmy and veer around them. I've been in a situation like this before, in Liverpool Street, when I was trying to escape with Sister Clare of the Shnax, so I put that experience to good use.

A sprawling zombie – he looks like he was a construction worker when he was alive – grabs my left leg just above my ankle and pulls me down. I kick out at him as I fall and he slides away from me. I realise he has no legs – they look like they were torn from him at the knees when he was turned – which is why he's lying on the floor.

Taking advantage of my unexpected fall, I slip through the legs of a couple of zombies ahead of me. One is a woman in a miniskirt. I grab hold of the skirt and spin her around, so that she clatters into several other zombies and knocks them over. As the skirt rips, I let her go, propel myself to my feet and carry on.

Rage has found a way through the press of zombies around him and has picked up speed. He calls cheerfully to me, 'This is the life, isn't it?'

I ignore him and stay focused on the reviveds, ducking their grasping fingers, kicking out at them, looking for open channels that I can exploit.

Master Zhang is trailing us, slowly, as if out for a Sunday stroll. He watches calmly, but not too curiously. I guess he's seen all this lots of times before.

A girl my own sort of age grabs the rucksack on my back

and tries to wrestle it from me, either realising that the smell is coming from there, or simply seeing it as the best way to slow me down. I turn sharply and slam the flat of my palm up into her chin, snapping her head back and knocking her loose.

'An interesting move,' Master Zhang says. 'Most people in your position would have simply punched her.'

I don't reply. There's no time. Before the girl staggers away from me, I grab her and force her to her knees. Then I step on to her back and launch myself forward, flying over the heads of a pack of zombies who were closing in on me.

'Oh, now even I've got to applaud that one,' Rage booms, clapping loudly. He's been forced to a standstill close to where I land. 'How about we do this as a team?' he bellows, offering me his hand.

'Get stuffed,' I snap, and look for another small zombie that I can use as a springboard.

This time, as I'm hurling myself into the air, one of the reviveds catches hold of my left foot and hauls me to the floor. A cluster of them press in around me, fingers clawing at my face, trying to rip my head open, to get to the juicy brain which they think is the source of the smell.

'No!' I scream, pushing them back and struggling to my feet. I look around desperately, hoping that Master Zhang will help. But he just stands there, gazing at me, challenging me with his expression to figure my own way out of this mess.

Rage is moving forward again. He's snapped an arm off one of the zombies and is using it as a club, lashing out at anyone within range. Many of the zombies who get knocked back by him shake their heads, then refocus on me, figuring I offer easier pickings. A huge crowd of them starts to close in around me.

'Sod this,' I pant, knowing my number's up if I don't act swiftly.

Wriggling free of the rucksack, I rip it open and start throwing slivers of brain around, as if it was some weird kind of confetti. When the zombies spot the grey chunks, they go wild, but now they're concentrating on the bits of brain, trying to catch them as I toss them about, emptying the rucksack as quickly as I can.

When the rucksack is clean, I let it drop and fall still, letting the zombies see that I'm not trying to escape, that I have no need to run, that I'm the same as them.

A few of the reviveds sniff me suspiciously, growling like dogs, but then they leave me be and tear the remains of the rucksack to shreds, trying to squeeze out any last morsels of brain that might be hidden in the folds.

I look up at Master Zhang, shamefully, as the zombies part around me, but he's following Rage, no longer interested in me. I think about heading back to County Hall, or maybe just slipping away completely, figuring that's the end of my career as an Angel. But I want to see what happens to Rage. I'm hoping he'll brick it like I did and cast his rucksack aside.

But Rage is like a wrecking ball. The zombies slow him down, but they can't stop him. He slaps them back with the arm, punches and kicks them when the arm is no longer any good, sticks his head down and forces his way forward, refusing to accept defeat. I almost cheer on the rampaging brute, but then I recall how he killed Dr Cerveris and deserted the rest of the zom heads, and I hold my tongue.

He finally makes it to the end of the concourse and squeezes through the exit. As soon as he's out, he tears off the rucksack and lobs it back inside the station. The reviveds scurry after it, quickly losing interest in him, as they lost it in me.

'Now *that* was fun,' Rage grins as we join him outside. He wipes blood – not his own – from his face. 'I guess some of us have what it takes, Becky, and some of us don't.'

'Bite me,' I snarl, then cast a miserable look at Master Zhang. 'I guess this means I've had it.'

'Not at all,' he says, surprising both of us.

'What are you talking about?' Rage snaps. 'She failed.'

'No,' Zhang says. 'The test is designed to measure one's bravery, ingenuity and strength, but also one's level of common sense. Almost no novice Angel has made it all the way across the concourse. In fact you are only the third, and the other two made it with cunning and speed, not sheer muscle power.'

'Sweet!' Rage beams, thrilled with himself.

'So . . . I didn't fail?' I frown.

'No. You showed that you were willing to face adversity, and you handled yourself well. In fact you made it further than most. But just as importantly, when you realised you could go no further, you were sensible enough to rid yourself of the beacon which was attracting the reviveds. Those who fail are those who break too early with fear, or those who lack the wit to throw away the rucksack.'

'Then I did better than Rage, in a way,' I joke.

'In your dreams,' Rage grunts.

'There is no better or worse in my eyes,' Master Zhang says. 'You both passed. That is the end of the matter.'

With that, he heads back to County Hall, but circles round the rear of the station this time, rather than return through the concourse. Rage slides up beside me as we trail our mentor. He points to himself and says, 'One of three.' Then he points to me and says, 'One of *who cares?*'

He laughs and moves on before I can reply, leaving me to scowl angrily at his back with a mixture of hatred, jealousy and grudging respect.

NINETEEN

Master Zhang leads Rage and me back to the room in County Hall where I was training earlier. He says that since he has both of us with him, he will train with the pair of us for the rest of the session.

I get excited when I hear that. After passing our Waterloo-based test, I assume that we're ready to move on, that he'll start teaching us complicated moves. But it's business as usual, the only change being that he now takes turns to throw us to the floor. I'm pleased to see that Rage is treated the same way I am, but disappointed that Master Zhang isn't taking us a few stages further forward.

We've been back about an hour when the door opens and Dr Oystein steps into the room. He's not alone. Ashtat, Carl, Shane and Jakob are with him, as well as a man I recognise but didn't expect to see here.

'Mr Burke?' I gasp.

'Hello again, B,' my ex-teacher says, as our training draws to a halt. 'We seem to keep meeting in the strangest of places, don't we?'

As I gawp at my old teacher, I recall what Reilly said about seeing someone he knew with a pack of Angels after he'd deserted the army following the riots in the underground complex, and it starts to make sense.

Billy Burke had worked in the complex with Reilly, but he'd never seemed to fit in with the soldiers and scientists. Of them all, only he truly cared about the welfare of the zom heads. That was why they'd recruited him, to help them with the sometimes rebellious teenagers.

I should have figured this out before. Having severed his ties with the army, Reilly wouldn't have wanted to approach any of his old crew. Burke was different. Reilly wouldn't have considered him the same as the others. He'd have felt he could trust the compassionate counsellor.

'Josh told me he'd released you,' Burke says as I stand, staring at him silently. 'I was hoping you'd find your way here. That's why I passed on your description to Dr Oystein.'

I frown. '*You* told the doc about me?'

'Yes,' Dr Oystein answers. 'That is how I knew your name when you first came here, and some of your background.'

I scratch my ear. 'I thought Reilly spotted me on the cameras and told you.'

The doctor shakes his head. 'No. It was Billy.'

285

'Well . . . thanks . . . I guess,' I mutter, lowering my hand.

'It is good to see you again, B,' Dr Oystein says. 'You have settled in nicely, I hear.'

'I'm doing all right,' I sniff.

'Zhang,' Dr Oystein says, bowing towards our mentor.

Master Zhang bows in return.

'How did our pair of fledgling Angels fare with their test earlier?' Dr Oystein asks.

'They passed,' Zhang says simply, giving us no more credit than that.

'I told you they would,' Burke smiles. 'They're a rare pair, those two.'

'Some of us are rarer than others,' Rage says, cocking an eyebrow at me.

'Why don't you shut up for once?' I snarl.

'Who's gonna make me?' Rage growls, squaring up to me.

'I would rather you did not fight,' Dr Oystein says quietly, and Rage immediately goes all sheepish and shuffles his feet.

'Sorry,' he mutters.

'Oh, isn't he a good boy,' I coo, then spit with contempt, which isn't easy with my dry mouth. 'Don't trust him, Dr Oystein. He's only buttering you up to make you like him, the same way he did with Dr Cerveris.'

'Why should I?' Rage counters. 'Dr Oystein hasn't tried to cage me up like those other buggers did. I'm free to leave whenever I please.'

'And you will,' I snort. 'When it suits you. And you'll probably kill a few of us along the way, just for the hell of it.'

Rage shrugs and turns to Dr Oystein. 'I told you, when I saw her in the lab, that she'd have nothing good to say about me.'

'Yes, you did,' the doctor nods. 'And B has warned us to be wary of you. I have chosen to ignore both of your opinions, so please save your bickering for another time. You are going to be room-mates, so you will have plenty of –'

'You're not sticking him in with us!' I shout.

'Please, B, there is no need to raise your voice.'

'But –'

'Please,' Dr Oystein says again. The fact that he sounds as if he is actually asking, rather than issuing an order, slows me in my tracks. I grumble something beneath my breath but otherwise hold my tongue.

Carl and the others are watching our exchange with interest, eyeing up Rage.

'This is Michael Jarman,' Dr Oystein says to them. 'But he prefers –'

'*Michael Jarman?*' I laugh.

'You didn't think I was christened Rage, did you?' he says.

'I brought you here to meet him, because Rage will be sharing your room if nobody has any objections,' Dr Oystein continues, then smiles fleetingly at me. 'With the noted exception of Miss Smith.'

'If he moves in, I'm moving out,' I say stiffly.

Dr Oystein sighs. 'That would be regrettable. I let everyone decide where they want to room once they have adjusted to life here, but I prefer to assign places to begin with. If you choose not to respect my decision, I will take that as a sign that you do not trust my judgement.'

'No, it's not that . . . I mean I don't . . .' I growl with frustration. 'He's a killer. He betrayed me and the other zom heads.'

'I know.'

'But you want to stick him in with me anyway?'

'Yes.'

Dr Oystein's expression never alters.

'Fine,' I grunt. 'Whatever.'

'Thank you,' he says and seeks the approval of the others. They shrug, knowing nothing about Rage or my beef with him. 'In that case, thank you for your time, and feel free to return to your usual duties. B and Rage, would you please accompany Mr Burke and myself on a short walk? There are certain matters I wish to discuss with the pair of you.'

'Sure,' I say, shooting Rage an evil look. He only smirks in return.

We file out, Dr Oystein and Burke in front, Rage and me a few steps behind, keeping as far apart from one another as we can.

TWENTY

We wind our way through the corridors of County Hall, Dr Oystein taking his time. Burke looks back at me. 'I was so relieved when Josh said that he'd spared you.'

'Yeah, well, I was the only one he did spare,' I say bitterly, recalling how he torched the other zom heads.

Burke looks contrite. 'If I'd been there, I would have tried to stop him.'

'Really?' I challenge him. 'You seemed to be fine with what he was doing the rest of the time.'

My old teacher sighs heavily. 'I'm sorry for all of the deception and lies. They thought I was on their side. They knew I didn't approve of everything they were doing, but they had no idea I was in league with Dr Oystein. I had to play ball or they might have become suspicious.'

'You were a spy?' I frown.

'Yes.'

'I do not trust the military,' Dr Oystein says without pausing or turning. 'They wish to restore order to the world, which is my wish too, but they want to do so on their own terms. We must be wary of them. They include me in some of their plans and experiments, since they respect my specialist knowledge of the undead, but I like to keep track of all that I am excluded from too. Billy agreed to act as my inside man, as he had already earned their trust before our paths crossed.'

'You mean you were working for the army before you met Dr Oystein?'

Burke nods.

'Not especially loyal, are you?' I snort.

'I'm loyal to those I deem deserving of loyalty,' he says sharply.

Silence falls again. We exit the building on to the riverbank. I think for a second that Dr Oystein plans to take us bowling, but then I see that he's heading for the aquarium. 'Was the story about you convincing Josh and the others to feed me and keep me revitalised the truth?' I ask Burke.

'Yes,' he says.

'Thanks,' I mutter.

'No need. You would have done the same for me.' I raise an eyebrow and Burke chuckles wryly. 'Well, I like to tell myself that you would.'

We share a quick grin, then we're stepping off the path

into the dim, silent world of the aquarium. I came here in the past, but not since I rocked up at County Hall as a zombie. I hadn't even thought about this place. Fish have been among the last things on my mind recently.

I find, to my surprise, that most of the tanks are still in working order, teeming with underwater life as they were before.

'Do zombies eat fish brains?' I ask.

'Only those of a certain size,' Dr Oystein says. 'We thrive primarily on human brains, but those of larger animals and fish are nourishing too. Fortunately a small band of people managed to drive back the zombies on the day of the attack and barricade themselves in here. Ciara was one of them. They survived and hung on until we set up camp in County Hall. All except Ciara chose to be relocated to compounds beyond the city once we gave them that option. She had grown fond of the place, and of my Angels, so she decided to stay.'

We move in silence from one tank to another, studying an array of fish, turtles, squid and all sorts of weird species. Many are beautifully coloured and strangely shaped, and I'm reminded of how exotic this place seemed when I came here as a child. I never saw the appeal of aquariums before I visited. I thought they were dull places for nerds who loved goldfish.

We come to a glass tunnel through a huge tank of sharks.

There are other things in there with them, but who takes notice of anything else when you spot a shark?

Dr Oystein draws to a halt in the middle of the tunnel and gazes around. 'I did not know much about the maintenance of aquariums when I first moved in, but I have made it my business to learn. Some of my Angels share my passion and tend to the tanks in my absence. Perhaps one of you will wish to help too.'

Rage shakes his head. 'I only like fish when it's in batter and served up with chips.'

'Philistine,' I sneer.

'Up yours,' he says. 'They don't do anything for me. I'd rather go on safari than deep-sea diving.'

'I doubt if anyone will be going on safari any time in the near future,' Dr Oystein murmurs. 'And the zoos have been picked clean of their stock by now — I sent teams to check, in case we could harvest more brains. But at least this small part of our natural heritage survives.'

Dr Oystein sits down and nods for us to join him on the floor. He says nothing for a moment, relishing the underwater world which we've become a temporary part of. Then he makes a happy sighing sound.

'For many decades I have found God in the creatures of the sea,' he says. 'The sheer diversity of life, the crazy shapes and colours, the way they can adapt and flourish ... I defy anyone to stroll through an aquarium and tell me our world could throw forth such wonders without the guiding hand of a higher power.'

'You're not a fan of Darwin then?' Rage snickers.

'Oh, I believe in evolution,' Dr Oystein says. 'But you do not have to exclude one at the expense of the other. All creatures – ourselves included – are servants of nature and the changing forces of the world in which we live. But how can such a world have come into being by accident? If evolution was the only force at work, large, dull, powerful beasts would have prevailed and stamped their mark on this planet long ago. Only a curious, playful God would have populated our shores and seas with such a glittering, spellbinding array of specimens.'

Dr Oystein turns his gaze away from the sharks to look us in the eye, one after the other, as he speaks.

'I did not bring you here by chance. As I said, I find God in places like this, and God is what I wish to discuss. I was not always a believer, so I will not be dismayed if you do not share my beliefs. I am not looking to convert either of you, merely to explain how and why I came to put together my team of Angels.

'I was born shortly after the turn of the twentieth century. It might seem odd, but I no longer recall the exact date. It is even possible that I was born in the late nineteenth century, though I do not think I am quite that old.

'For the first thirty-five or forty years of my life, I was an atheist. I hurled the works of Darwin and other scientists at those who clung to the ways of what I thought was a ridiculous, outdated past. Then, in the 1930s, in the lead-up to the Second World War, God found me and I realised what a fool I had been.' Dr Oystein lowers his gaze and sighs again, sadly this time.

'God found me,' he repeats in a cracked voice, 'but not before the Nazis found me first . . .'

TWENTY-ONE

Dr Oystein travelled around Europe with his parents when he was a child. As a man, he continued to tour the world, but ended up settling in Poland, where his wife was from and where his elder brother – also a doctor – had set up home.

They were happy years, he tells us, the brothers working together, raising their families, enjoying the lull between the wars. Dr Oystein and his brother were noted geneticists who could have lived anywhere – they had offers from across the globe – but they were happy in Poland.

Then the Nazis invaded. Dr Oystein's instincts told him to flee, but his wife and children didn't want to leave their home and his brother refused to go too. With an uneasy feeling, he agreed to remain and hoped that he would be allowed to carry on his work in peace and quiet, since he had no strong political ties and wasn't a member of any of the religions or races which the Nazis despised.

Unfortunately for the doctor, the Nazis were almost as interested in genetics as they were in killing Jews and gypsies. They were intent on improving the human form and creating a master race. They saw Dr Oystein and his brother as key allies in their quest to overcome the weaknesses of nature.

When Dr Oystein rejected their advances, he was imprisoned in a concentration camp along with his brother and their families. The camps weren't as hellish as the death camps which were built later in the war, but the chances of survival were slim all the same.

'If the guards disliked you,' Dr Oystein says quietly, 'they worked you until you could work no more, then executed you for failing to complete your tasks. Or they tortured you until you confessed to whatever crime they wished to charge you with. They might make you stand still for hours on end, under the threat of death if you moved, then shoot you when you collapsed from sheer exhaustion.'

Dr Oystein had three children. His brother had four. The Nazis killed one of Dr Oystein's children and two of his brother's, and made it clear that their wives and the surviving children would be executed as well if the brothers didn't do as they were told. When they saw what they were up against, they agreed to be shipped off to a secret unit to work for their monstrous new masters.

The Nazis yearned to unravel the secrets of life and death,

to bring the dead back from beyond the grave. There were two reasons. One was to create an army of undead soldiers, to give them an advantage in the war. The other was so that they could survive forever, to indefinitely enjoy the pleasures of the new society which they were hell-bent on creating.

Dr Oystein and his brother were part of an elite team, some of the greatest minds in the world, all working towards the same warped goal. Some were there by force, some by choice. It didn't matter. They all had to slave away as hard as they could. Nazis were not known for their tolerance of failure.

'We made huge strides forward,' Dr Oystein says without any hint of pride. 'We unlocked secrets which are still beyond the knowledge of geneticists today. If we had been allowed to share our findings with the world, we would have been hailed as wonders and people of your generation would be benefiting from our discoveries. But the Nazis were self-ish. Records of our advances were buried away in mounds of paperwork, far from prying eyes.'

Dr Oystein created the first revived. He brought a woman back to life after she had died of malnutrition in a concentration camp. (He says that most of their cadavers were drawn from the camps.)

'It should have been a wondrous moment,' he whispers. 'I had done what only God had previously achieved. Mankind's potential skyrocketed. The future opened up to us as it never had before. Immortality – or at least a vastly extended life – became ours for the taking.'

But instead he felt wretched, partly because he knew the Nazis would take his discovery and do terrible things with it, but also because he felt that he had broken the laws of the universe, and he was sure that nothing good could come of that.

The Nazis rejoiced. The revived was a mindless, howling, savage beast, of no practical use to them, but they were confident that the doctor and his team would build on this breakthrough and find a way to restore the mind as well as the body. But they couldn't. No matter how many corpses they brought back to life, they couldn't get the brains to work. Every zombie was a drooling, senseless wreck.

'The Nazis discussed dropping the living dead behind enemy lines,' Dr Oystein says, 'but as vicious as they were, they were not fools. They knew they could not manage the spread of the reviveds once they released them, and they had no wish to inherit a world of deadly, infectious zombies.'

Dr Oystein was sure that they had pushed the project as far as they could. He didn't share that view with the Nazis, but all of his results suggested to him that they had come to a dead end. He didn't think the brain of a corpse could ever be restored.

While all this was happening, the Nazis kept presenting the brothers with regular reports of their wives and children, photographs and letters to prove that they were alive and well. One day that stopped. They were told that the information was being withheld until they created a revitalised specimen, but the doctors were afraid that something terrible had happened.

'And we were right,' Dr Oystein mutters. 'I found out much later that both of my remaining children had died. My wife went wild and attacked those who had imprisoned her. My brother's wife tried to pull her away, to calm her down.

'The women were shot by an over-eager guard. That left only my brother's daughter and son. The girl died a couple of years later, but the boy survived.' Dr Oystein coughs and looks away. 'I thought of my nephew often over the decades but never sought him out. I didn't want him to see what I had become.'

With no news of their loved ones, and fearing the worst, the brothers made up their minds to escape. They hated working for the Nazis, and if their families had been executed, they had nothing to lose — their own lives didn't matter to them. They put a lot of time and thought into their plan, and almost pulled it off. But their laboratory was one of the most highly guarded prisons in the world. Luck went against them on the night of their escape. They were caught and tortured.

Under interrogation, Dr Oystein told the Nazis that he thought it was impossible to revitalise a subject, that the vacant zombies in their holding cells were as good as it was ever going to get. The Nazis were furious. They decided to teach the brothers a vicious lesson, to serve as an example. They infected the pair with the undead gene and turned them into zombies.

'That should have been the end of us,' Dr Oystein says, eyes distant as he remembers that dark, long-ago day. 'But there was something nobody had counted on. Like every other revived, I could not be brought back to consciousness by the hand of man. But there was another at work, a doctor of sorts, whose power was far greater than mine or anyone else's.

'Mock me if you wish – many others have before you, and for all I know they are right – but I am certain that my mind and soul were restored by a force of ultimate good, a force I choose to call *God*.'

TWENTY-TWO

Dr Oystein pauses to study the sharks. I glance around at the others, disturbed by what I've been told. Burke returns my gaze calmly, giving no sign whether he buys this or not. Rage is more direct. He puts a finger to the side of his head and twirls it around — *cuckoo!* But I can tell by the way he peeks guiltily at Dr Oystein as he lowers his arm that the story has troubled him too.

'God spoke to me when He saved me,' Dr Oystein continues. 'He told me what had happened, why I had been spared, what I must do.'

The reviveds were kept in holding pens, secure but not foolproof. Plenty of security measures were in place, but all had been designed with the limitations of brainless subjects in mind. The Nazis hadn't considered the threat of a conscious, intelligent zombie.

Dr Oystein freed the reviveds and set them on the soldiers

and scientists, who were taken by surprise. Nobody was spared. The zombies ran riot, killing or converting everyone, helped by the doctor, who opened doors and sought out hiding places.

When all of the humans had been disposed of, Dr Oystein destroyed every last scrap of paperwork and evidence of what had been going on. He knew that reports had been sent to officials elsewhere, but he did what he could to limit the damage. After that, with a heavy heart, he killed all of the zombies one by one, ripping out their brains to ensure they were never brought back to life again.

Dr Oystein doesn't mention his brother, but I'm sure he must have killed him too. I'm not surprised that he doesn't go into specifics. It's not the sort of thing I imagine you want to spend a lot of time thinking about.

His work finished, Dr Oystein slipped away into the night, to set about the mission which he had been given by the voice inside his head.

God told Dr Oystein that the human race had become too violent and destructive. Bringing the dead back to life was the final straw. There had to be a reckoning, like when the Bible said that He flooded the world. A thinning of the ranks. A cleansing.

The voice told Dr Oystein that there would be a plague of zombies in the near future. On a day of divine destiny, a war would break out between mankind and the living dead.

'Are you saying God unleashed the zombies?' I ask incredulously, unable to keep quiet any longer.

'Of course not,' Dr Oystein replies. 'But God saw that scientists would conduct fresh experiments and create new strains of the zombie gene. And one day one of them would accidentally or deliberately release an airborne strain which would sweep the globe and convert millions of humans into undead monsters. He could have spared us the agony if He had wished, but honestly, B, can you think of any good reason why He should have intervened?'

'Lots of innocent people died,' I mutter.

Dr Oystein nods. 'They always do. That is the nature of our world. But do you think it was a perfect society, that our leaders were just and good, that as a race we were not guilty of unimaginable, unpardonable crimes?'

'You can't punish everyone for the sins of a few,' Rage growls.

'Of course you can,' Dr Oystein says. 'Just step outside and look around if you do not believe that. As a people, we offended our creator and turned on our own like jackals. We soiled this world. Was the plague of zombies a harsh judgement? Perhaps. But unfair? I think not.'

Dr Oystein shakes his head when nobody says anything else, then continues.

He criss-crossed the world in the years to come, building up contacts among all sorts of officials. His first priority was to crack down on undead outbreaks, and to contain them when they happened. With the help of his contacts, he kept the existence of zombies a secret. Rumours trickled out every so often, but nobody in their right mind paid any attention to them. Hollywood film makers were paid to weave wild tales about the living dead, to turn them into movie monsters, like Dracula or the Mummy.

But no matter how hard he worked, the experiments continued. Nazi scientists in hiding created their own small zombie armies in the hope of launching a bid to control the world again. Some sold their secrets to rich men or leaders in countries where power struggles were a way of life.

Dr Oystein experimented too. God had told him that he would need to fight fire with fire if he was to have any chance of redeeming the human race. The doctor was the first of what could be a highly effective force of revitaliseds. If he could find a way to restore others, the world might regain a sliver of hope.

'Although it repulsed me, I returned to my work,' he says, hanging his head with shame. 'If there was any other way, I would have seized it gladly, but there wasn't.'

'What makes you think you're any better than the rest of the creeps then?' I sneer. 'Maybe the airborne gene was created by one of *your* associates, using technology that *you* pioneered.'

'Perhaps,' Dr Oystein nods. 'But I do not think that is the

case. I have learnt much about the gene over the decades, but the airborne strain was new to me. It is a destructive strain, while my work has been focused on the positive possibilities, on the human mind and its restoration.

'I finally figured out a way to create revitaliseds,' he goes on. 'I hoped to perfect a vaccine that would stop people returning to life when they were infected — if zombies could only kill, not convert, they would be far easier to deal with. Failing that, I hoped to provide the undead with the ability to recover their wits, so that they could be reasoned with.

'Until that point I had experimented solely on corpses or on those who had been revived. But if prevention was to serve as the key to our survival, it meant I would have to –'

'– experiment on living people,' Rage cuts in, beating Dr Oystein to the punch. He doesn't look outraged, simply fascinated.

'You're sick,' I snarl, but for once I'm not insulting Rage. My comment is directed at Dr Oystein. I rise and glare at him. 'You're just like the Nazis and the scientists who were experimenting on the zom heads.'

'I do not claim to be any nobler than them,' Dr Oystein says softly. 'I have done many dreadful things and you have every right to vilify me.'

'Then why shouldn't I?' I snap. 'You said I was an Angel. You offered protection and told me we could do good. Why should I accept the word of a man who experimented on living people and probably killed more than a few in the process?'

'Many have died at my hands over the years,' he admits. 'I see their faces every night, even though I don't dream.'

'So why should I pledge myself to you?' I press. 'Why shouldn't I storm out of here and never look back?'

Dr Oystein shrugs. 'Because I was successful,' he whispers. 'I found a way to revitalise zombies.'

Now it's my turn to shrug. 'So? Does that mean we should forgive you?'

Dr Oystein looks up at last. There's no anger in his gaze, only misery. 'I am not worthy of forgiveness, but I do think that I am worthy of your support.'

'Why?' I ask again, barking the question this time.

'Because I created you,' Dr Oystein says. And as I stare at him, trying to figure out what he means, he says, 'Tell me, B, do you have a little c-shaped scar on your upper right thigh?'

In the silence that follows, all I can do is stare at him, then through the glass walls of the tunnel at the sharks circling patiently, their wide mouths lifting at the corners, almost in wicked, mocking smiles.

TWENTY-THREE

I've had the c-shaped scar since I was two or three years old. I was injected with an experimental flu vaccine. It worked a treat and I've never had so much as a sniffle since. I sometimes thought it was odd that the vaccine hadn't taken off — nobody else I knew had been vaccinated with it. I figured there must have been side effects which I'd been lucky enough to avoid.

'Haven't you wondered why virtually all of the revitaliseds are teenagers?' Burke asks softly.

I stare at him, thinking back. In the underground complex I never saw any adult revitaliseds. I assumed they were being held in a different section, that we'd been grouped together by age.

Apart from Dr Oystein and Master Zhang, they're all teenagers or younger here in County Hall too. Dr Oystein told me that adult revitaliseds were rare, but I never pushed it any further than that. I've got so used to being around others my own age that it didn't seem strange.

'I developed the vaccine about forty years ago,' Dr Oystein says. 'It is unpredictable and does not work in everyone. Many who have been vaccinated do not recover their senses when infected. Those who revitalise do so at different rates. The fastest has been eighteen hours. At six months, you are one of the slowest.'

'See?' Rage smiles. 'You're slow. It's official.'

I ignore him and stay focused on Dr Oystein.

'My intention was to have teams vaccinate every living person before the wave of reviveds broke across the world. But the vaccine was unstable. It could not be held in check indefinitely. If a person was not bitten by a zombie, after fifteen or so years it turned on its host. The body broke down. The bones and flesh liquefied. It was swift – from start to finish, no more than half a day – and incredibly painful.'

'You're telling me that if I hadn't been attacked by zombies, I'd have ended up as a puddle of goo in another year or two?' I gasp.

The doctor nods and I laugh bitterly.

'You're some piece of work, doc. The Nazis had nothing on you.'

He flinches at the insult.

'But now that we've been infected . . .' Rage says.

'The vaccine will not harm us while it is fighting with the

zombie gene,' Dr Oystein says. 'We are safe now that we have revitalised.

'If I had known when the day of reckoning was due, I could have vaccinated as many people as possible,' he continues. 'But God never revealed the date to me. If I had miscalculated, I could have wiped out the entire race by myself, no zombies required.'

Rage whistles softly. 'That's some crazy power. Were you ever tempted to . . . you know . . . just for the hell of it?'

We all stare at him.

'Come on,' he protests. 'You guys were thinking the same thing. If you had the world in the palm of your hand, and all you had to do was squeeze . . .'

'You're a sick, twisted bastard,' I sneer.

'No,' Dr Oystein says. 'Rage is right. I *was* tempted. But not in the way he thinks. I had no interest in crushing nations. I was tempted because I was afraid. I knew the terrors and hardships we must face, and I did not want to embrace such a future. It would have been easier to condemn mankind to a swift, certain end, to accept defeat and ensure that nobody need suffer the agonies of a long, drawn-out war of nightmarish proportions. Death by vaccine would have been simpler, the coward's way out.

'I am various low, despicable things,' Dr Oystein whispers, 'but I do not think I am a coward. I am guilty of many foul crimes, but I have always accepted my responsibilities. I

309

ignored the pleas of my weaker self and remained true to my calling. If mankind is to perish, it will not be because I was found wanting.'

Dr Oystein rises and starts walking. The rest of us head after him. He moves faster than before, striding through the aquarium, leading us out into the open. On the riverbank he hurries to the wall overlooking the Thames and bends over it as if about to throw up.

'I'm sorry,' he moans, but it's unclear whether he's apologising to us or the souls of the people he experimented on and killed over the course of his long and dreadful life.

TWENTY-FOUR

Dr Oystein stays facing the river for a couple of minutes while the rest of us stand back, waiting for him to recover.

'This guy needs to see a shrink,' Rage murmurs.

I turn to rip into him for being an insensitive pig, but I see by his expression that he wasn't having a dig. The big, ugly lump looks about as pitying as he ever could.

'I doubt if any ordinary professional could help him,' Burke says softly. 'This isn't a normal complaint. To have endured all that he has ... I'm stunned he's not a gibbering wreck.'

'Do you believe everything he told us?' I ask. 'About Nazis, God, all that ...' I was about to say *crap* but decide that's not the right word, ' ... stuff?'

'We'll discuss that later,' Burke says and nods at Dr Oystein, who is turning from the river at last. He looks embarrassed.

'My apologies. Sometimes the guilt overwhelms me. I know that I have done what was asked of me, but there are days when that does not seem like a justifiable excuse. God did not authorise the experiments, the tests that went awry, the lives which I have sacrificed. I see no other way that I could have proceeded, but still I wonder ... and fear.'

He sighs and glances up at the London Eye, turning as smoothly as ever, the pods shining brightly against the backdrop of the cloudy sky.

'So why are all of your Angels teenagers?' I ask, to draw him back to what he was talking about earlier. 'Why didn't you vaccinate adults too?'

'I felt that children would be more appropriate,' Dr Oystein says. 'They are, generally speaking, more innocent and pure of heart than adults.'

'You wouldn't think like that if you'd gone to my school,' I mutter, and share a grin with Mr Burke.

Dr Oystein smiles ruefully. 'That was not the only factor. There were practical reasons too. Children were easier to vaccinate than adults — they received so many jabs that nobody took notice of one more. And since their bodies were undergoing natural changes during growth, they were better equipped to contain the vaccine — children generally held out a few years longer than grown-ups before succumbing to the side effects.

'Also, I distrusted adults. They were set in their ways, less

312

open to fresh ideas and change. I needed soldiers who would think nothing of their own lives, who would dedicate themselves entirely to the cause. I decided that children were more likely to answer such a demanding call.

'Every year my team vaccinated a selection from newborns to teenagers in cities, towns and villages across the world. Every time I looked at the files – and I made a point of acknowledging each and every subject – I suffered a conflict of interests. I found myself hoping that the plague would strike soon, to spare the vaccinated children the painful death they would have to endure if it did not, yet also wishing that it wouldn't, because that would mean so many more people dying.'

Dr Oystein falls silent again, remembering some of the faces of the damned.

'How many did you vaccinate each year?' I ask.

'Several thousand,' he says. 'Always in a different area, with a fresh team under a different guise, to avert people's suspicions.'

'What do you mean?' Rage frowns.

'One year we offered a cure for the flu,' Dr Oystein explains. 'The next year we promoted a measles vaccine. The year after something to help prevent AIDS. Each time we hid behind a fake company or charity.'

'So if you've been doing this for decades . . .' I try to do the maths.

'Hundreds of thousands,' Dr Oystein says softly.

'How the hell do you cover up that many deaths?' I explode. 'Especially if they melted down into muck. I never read about anything like that in the Sunday papers.'

'As I already explained, I had contacts in high places,' Dr Oystein says. 'They clamped down on any talk that might have compromised our position.'

'Still,' I mutter, '*somebody* must have leaked word of what was going on.'

'They did,' Burke says. 'It was all over the place, in self-published books and on the internet. I remember coming across articles back when I knew nothing about Dr Oystein or his work. Like any sane person, I dismissed them. Who could believe stories of a drug that made people melt?'

'Truth is stranger than fiction,' Rage says smugly, as if he's just come out with an incredibly original, witty line.

'All right,' I mutter. 'I'm getting it. You vaccinated thousands of kids every year to create an army of revitaliseds when the Apocalypse hit. So there must be, what, a few hundred thousand of us, ranging in age from adults down to babies?'

'Less,' Dr Oystein says. 'Many failed to revitalise, particularly those who had matured. Others were slaughtered during the assaults and their brains were eaten. Young children who revitalised either failed to follow the signs to my safe houses or reverted due to not being able to feed.

'We cannot be sure, but we think there are maybe a couple of thousand Angels worldwide, possibly less.'

'You didn't get a great return for all those sacrifices, did you, doc?' Rage asks quietly.

'No,' the doctor says, even quieter.

'And are there centres like this in different countries, full of Angels?' I ask.

'Yes,' Dr Oystein says hesitantly.

'Something wrong with the others?' I press.

'No. But they are not as important as the Angels in London.'

I laugh shortly. 'I bet your people say that to all the Angels.'

He shakes his head. 'We are in a unique position. Several of the revitaliseds who came to us here asked to be relocated once I revealed what I am about to reveal to you.'

'That sounds ominous,' Rage growls but his face is alight with curiosity. I bet mine is too. I haven't a clue what's coming next or how it can be any worse than what he's told us already.

'This is a universe of good and evil,' Dr Oystein says. 'I am sure you know from your lessons in school that for every action there is an equal and opposite reaction.'

'Quit with the dramatic build-up, doc,' Rage huffs. 'Give it to us straight.'

'Very well,' the doctor says as a rare angry spark flashes

across his eyes. 'Just as there is an ultimate force of good in this universe, there is also one of evil. To put it into the terms I find easiest to understand, God is real but so is Satan.'

Rage's smirk fades. I get a sick feeling in my stomach. Burke looks away.

'When God revitalised me, it was an act of love,' Dr Oystein says. 'He did it because He wished to hand mankind a lifeline. He was obliged to punish us, but He wanted to give us a fighting chance in the war to come.

'If God had left me to my own devices, I would have remained a mindless revived. Other scientists would have continued their experiments and the airborne strain of the disease would have been developed. When the ferocious undead arose, humanity would have lacked champions. The living need us. We can go where they can't, fight in ways they cannot.

'But there are laws which even God abides by. They are laws of His making, but if He ignores them, what use are they? A law which does not apply to all is no real sort of law.

'The forces of good and evil do not engage one another directly,' Dr Oystein continues. 'Their followers clash all the time, humanity forever swaying between the extremes of right and wrong, taking a positive step forward here, a negative step backward there. But God told me that if He or Satan ever takes a direct role in the affairs of man – if they

316

interfere in any way – then the other has the right to counteract that.'

'Tit for tat,' I whisper and Dr Oystein nods sombrely.

'That is why God so rarely reaches out to us. He might often wish to, when He looks down and sees us in pain, but He does not dare, because if He extends a hand of love, Satan can stretch forth a claw of hate.'

'This is bullshit,' I croak. 'It's madness.' I seek out Burke's gaze. 'Isn't it?' I shout.

Burke only shrugs uncomfortably.

'When God restored my consciousness,' Dr Oystein says, raising his voice ever so slightly, 'it allowed Satan to create his own mockery of the human form, a being of pure viciousness and spite who could wreak as much damage as I had the power to repair.

'I have sought long and hard for my demonic counterpart over the decades, but our paths never crossed. There were many occasions when I came close – and when he came close to tracking me down and striking at me, for he loathes me as much as I fear him – but something always kept us apart. Until now.'

Dr Oystein crosses his arms and trains his sights on me. 'You know evil's true name, don't you, B?'

'Get stuffed,' I whimper.

'Don't deny the truth. I can see the awareness in your eyes. Say it and spare me the unpleasant task. Please.'

'What the hell is he –' Rage starts to ask, but I blurt out the answer before he can finish.

'*Mr Dowling!*' I shout.

'Yes,' Dr Oystein says, shuddering. 'The clown with the smile of death. The creator of mutants and executioner of innocents. A creature of immense power and darkness, who relishes chaos and devastation, just like his grim master.

'Mr Dowling is the earthly representative of the force of ultimate evil. With the sinister clown's malevolent help, the Devil, as I call him, hopes to lead the zombies to victory and plunge our world into eternal, tormented night.

'The war between the living and the dead rages across the globe, but this is where it will be decided. London has been chosen as the key battleground. I set up base here for reasons I cannot define, and Mr Dowling has done likewise. The war we wage in this city of the damned will be the most instrumental of the conflict.

'We must take the fight to Mr Dowling,' Dr Oystein says, and his face betrays the terror he feels. 'He is our most direct and deadly nemesis. We will engage in a brutal, bloody battle to the death. If we triumph, peace and justice will reign and mankind can resume its quest to win heavenly favour.

'If we lose,' he concludes, and he doesn't need to drop his voice to make his sickening, dizzying point, 'every single one of us is damned and this world will become an outpost of Hell.'

To be continued ...

THE
ZOM-B
CHRONICLES

**TURN OVER
FOR A TASTE OF**

ZOM-B BABY

**HAVE YOU EVER HEARD AN UNDEAD
BABY SCREAM . . .?**

The baby keeps squealing, the same word repeated without even a pause for breath, calling for its *mummy*. The high-pitched noise cuts through me, making me wince and grind my teeth. Timothy is staring slack-jawed at the whining, red-eyed child.

'Make it stop,' I bark, covering my ears with my hands.

'How?' Timothy asks.

'Stick the spike back in its head.'

'No,' he says, face turning a shade paler at the thought. 'We can't do that. Let's find it a dummy.'

He lurches to a shelf stacked with baby stuff. He roots through the neat pile until he finds one. He hurries back and leans over the cot, cooing to the hellish baby, 'There, there. It's all right. We'll take care of you. No need to cry. Does it hurt? We'll make the pain go away. You're our little baby, aren't you?'

'Less of that crap,' I snort, shuddering at the thought of being mother to such an unearthly creature. 'Just shut the damn thing up.'

'Be nice, B,' Timothy tuts, then yelps and takes a quick step away from the cot. 'It tried to bite me!'

'Oh, give it to me,' I snap, nudging him aside and taking the dummy from him. I bend over, fingers of my left hand extended to widen the baby's mouth if necessary. Before I can touch its lips, the tiny creature's head shoots forward and its fangs snap shut on the bones sticking out of my middle and index fingers.

'Let go!' I roar with fright and try to pull my hand free. The baby rises with my arm, dangling from the bones, fangs locked into them, chewing furiously, head jerking left and right.

I wheel away from the cot, shaking my arm, trying to dislodge the monstrous infant. Timothy is yelling at me to be careful, not to drop the child. I swear loudly and try to hurl the baby loose.

I lose my balance, crash into the inflatable dinosaur and stumble to my knees. As I push myself to my feet again, the baby chews through the bones, drops to the floor and collapses on its back. It immediately resumes screaming for its mummy.

'Bloody hell!' I pant, retreating swiftly. My hand is trembling.

'I told you it wasn't a good idea,' Timothy says smugly. 'It obviously doesn't want a dummy, and with teeth like that, who are we to argue?'

'Sod what it wants,' I snarl. 'We have to shut it up.'

'You can try again if you wish,' Timothy chuckles. 'Personally I like my fingers the way they are. Those teeth are amazing. I wonder what they're made of?'

'You go on wondering,' I growl, crossing the room to pick up the spike. 'I'm putting a stop to this.'

'No,' Timothy says sternly. 'You can't do that.'

'I bloody well can,' I huff, advancing on the wailing baby.

Timothy steps in my way and crosses his arms.

'Move it, painter-boy. I'm not playing games.'

'Neither am I,' he says. 'You're not sticking that into the baby's head. You might kill it.'

'Do I look like I care?'

'No. That's why I can't let you proceed. You're not thinking clearly. You're upset and alarmed, understandably so. But when you calm down, you'll see that I'm right. This is a living baby, calling for its mother. It's afraid and lonely, probably in pain and shock. We have to comfort it, not treat it like a rabid animal that needs to be exterminated.'

'Didn't you see what it did with those teeth?' I roar, waving my gnawed fingerbones at him.

'Yes, but to be fair, you were attacking it. I would have bitten in self-defence too if you'd come at me like that.'

'But you wouldn't have been able to chew through my bones,' I note angrily.

'So its teeth are tougher than ours,' he shrugs. 'What of it? That's no reason to risk the poor thing's life. I can't let you stick that spike in again.'

'How are you going to stop me?' I challenge him.

'Just by standing here,' he says. 'You'll have to wrestle me out of the way to get to the baby. If you do that, you'll almost certainly scratch me. That would mean my death. I don't think you'd kill me so recklessly.'

'I'm a zombie,' I say softly, moving closer, going up on my toes to give him the evil eye. 'You don't know how my mind works, what I'd do if pushed.'

'Perhaps,' he says. 'But I'm willing to take that chance. This baby needs our help and love. It's our duty to study it, protect it, nurse it back to health. It can talk, so perhaps it can answer our questions when it recovers, tell us where it came from, what it is.'

'The babies never wanted to discuss much in my dreams,' I sniff. 'They only wanted to slaughter me.'

'But this isn't a dream,' Timothy says. 'The baby simply reacted the way any cornered creature would. Look at it lying there now, helpless as a ... well, as a *baby*. It doesn't pose a threat to us.'

I shake my head stubbornly. 'It's a monster. Of course it poses a threat.'

'You're a monster too,' Timothy smiles. 'But I'm not afraid of you and I'm not afraid of the baby either. We can be its foster parents.'

I stare at him oddly. 'What, become a couple?'

'Of course not,' he smiles. 'But we could be partners and raise it together.'

'Why would I want to do that?'

'Salvation,' he says softly, stepping aside when he sees me hesitate. 'My paintings have kept me busy, and I plan to carry on doing them for as long as I can. But I lost a lot that defined me as a human when the world fell. Maybe this baby is a way for me to retrieve some of my humanity, and for you too.

'I haven't been truly happy since the zombies took control. Content, yes, with my artistic output, but happy? No. I don't think you're happy either. This is a chance for us to put the darkness behind us for a while.'

'What if you're wrong?' I croak. 'What if the baby's as monstrous as it looks and only drags us further into trouble?'

Timothy shrugs. 'Isn't it worth taking that risk?'

I have a clear line of attack now. If I darted at the baby, Timothy wouldn't be able to stop me. I could smash its skull with the spike, crush its throat, rip it to pieces.

But how could I live with myself if I did that to a baby? I've sunk lower than I ever dreamt I could, murdered, scraped heads bare of their brains, lived among the fetid and the damned. But to butcher a baby just because I'm afraid of it, because I had nightmares about things like it when I was younger ...

'That freak will be the ruin of us both,' I pout.

'Perhaps,' Timothy grins, understanding from my expression that I can't follow through on my threat. 'But we have to take that chance. Now let's see what we can do to help this poor lamb. Maybe it will stop screaming if we put it back in its cot, tend to its wound and show that we mean no harm. I'm sure that with a little TLC it will respond to our ministrations and –'

Timothy stops. He had started to bend to pick up the baby, but now he turns and stares at the doorway, into the gloom of the large room beyond. He cocks his head and frowns.

'Do you hear that?' he whispers.

'What?'

I step up beside him, trying to focus. The screams of the baby – '*mummy. mummy. mummy*' – fill my head and I find it hard to tune them out.

Timothy moves through the doorway as if sleepwalking, eyes wide, a slight tic in his left cheek. I follow and close the door behind me, muffling the sounds of the baby.